Luna Rae is not Alone

Luna Rae is not Alone

HAYLEY WEBSTER

nosy
crow

First published in the UK in 2021 by Nosy Crow Ltd
The Crow's Nest, 14 Baden Place,
Crosby Row, London SE1 1YW

Nosy Crow and associated logos are trademarks and/or registered
trademarks of Nosy Crow Ltd

Text © Hayley Webster, 2021
Cover and chapter opener illustrations © Becky Thorn, 2021

The right of Hayley Webster to be identified as the author
of this work has been asserted.

ISBN: 978 1 78800 604 0

A CIP catalogue record for this book is available from
the British Library

Printed and bound in Great Britain by Clays Ltd, Elcograf S.p.A.
Typeset by Tiger Media

Paper

To any child who's ever felt
they have to keep a secret.

- H.W.

CHAPTER 1

The thing about a new house is everything's *new*.

That sounds really obvious, I know, but if you think about it, one of the things about where you live is that you build up all this stuff there. And not just stuff, *memories* linked to stuff. All the little ways things work, like the handle you had to push down twice to get into the bathroom, or the groove on the front step that if you went over it too fast you'd trip and land splat on your front. Or how far to open the window to let in enough fresh air so you can fall asleep but nobody could ever get in. Or the *smell*.

Good smells: baking, my mum's orange-oil perfume, the tomatoes in the greenhouse next to our old house.

Bad smells: ash trays, empty beer bottles, the paint they've used to decorate all the walls in the new house.

You get used to old things.

New things take getting used to.

"Memories don't go anywhere just because *you* do, Luna," Dad said. And I did get what he was saying. Moving doesn't mean any of the past ten years haven't happened, and it doesn't mean there won't be more good times, and it doesn't mean we can't make the new house even better than where we were before.

But.

Our new house is nothing like the old one. The old one was a mobile home in a field, with a massive vegetable garden, and things living underneath it. Penny Robinson at my old school said real houses don't have things living underneath them – *they are stuck to the ground, that's what real houses are, and they certainly don't move around from place to place, that's called a holiday.* But she was horrible and used to make stuff up about people, and I never liked her anyway.

I liked having a gap between the ground and our house. And I liked that it could move around, although we never really moved it much because Mum and Dad didn't want to leave the vegetable patch, and we never got asked to move on from there, so it felt safe. The sort of place that you'd look out of your bedroom window and sigh because you'd see a chaffinch or a squirrel or even an owl. Last summer me and Lolly used to crawl underneath it and see if we could hear Mum and Dad walking about above us. That was after Dad had got rid of the Great Plague (which is what

Mum called it). It was scary at the time, hearing these big rats under the house, scratching about and doing whatever it is rats do. Then Dad put traps under there, and poison, I think, and one sunny day came out from underneath holding all these dead furry things by their tails.

That bit wasn't very nice, actually.

It wasn't long after that he started talking about buying our new house. And Mum, well. Mum started being very quiet. I think she liked it there as much as I did but she never really talked to us about it.

I'm sitting on the kerb by the corner as you come into Ridgeway Close. Ours is the only truly finished street on the whole estate, and they've *spared no expense* in making it look like it's a really exclusive-but-homely place where you'll definitely want to live. It obviously worked on Mum and Dad, which means we are now the proud owners of number 16.

Number 14 is on the other side and is set out exactly the same as ours but the other way round, like our house is looking closely in a mirror. Nobody lives in number 14 yet, so I hope whoever moves in is nice. I think the walls are thin, though, so they'd better not have loads of rows or screaming, or crying, or breaking things in a huff and stomping up the stairs, because we'd hear all of it. Although noise *shouldn't* be a problem here, because everything is *up to the highest possible standards of building regulations*. It says so in the brochure.

"We're going to have trouble with all this open plan," said Mum when we first got the keys, standing in the dining room, which isn't a dining room because it's attached to the kitchen and the living room by two big plaster arches.

"It'll be nice," said Dad. "Communal."

"If I wanted communal, I'd live in a commune," said Mum.

"Ha ha!" said Dad, but Mum went out of the patio door to have a cigarette in the back garden, where she stood looking like someone in a painting, and Dad opened another can of beer.

Today Lolly had a half-day at her new school. We both start properly tomorrow. Dad is inside setting up the TV. I'm not sure when he's back at work at the warehouse, but he's saved up a month's holiday to arrange the move, and to help feel a bit better after not quite being himself for a while. But it's nice having him about every day, and I could get used to it. I don't tell him that because it might put too much pressure on him, and these days Dad doesn't cope very well with pressure.

I'm quite nosy, so I've already started making notes about the people I see on the close, what they're doing, what cars they drive, that sort of thing.

When I grow up I want to be a food writer, writing my own cookbooks with shiny covers. Or a detective. Or a Great Baker Detective. So, I have to get my practice in. I can't wait to bake in the new kitchen. It's bigger than our old one, and we have an actual fan oven. I'll have to change all the timings on my favourite recipes, though, which will take time and experimentation. The cooker at the old house was sort of on the wonk. Everything was hotter on one side. I had to customise the baking trays with little metal ramps. They're packed away now, somewhere, because I won't be needing them any more. Or if the new oven is on the wonk, what are the chances it will be on the wonk in exactly the same way?

The most interesting thing about Ridgeway

Close so far is that we have the Grande Homes Show Home on the corner opposite our house. It's a house that's done out with all the best furniture, all the best everything, to show people the sort of life they could have if they lived there. In the front garden are two huge flagpoles that rise way up into the sky, both with the bright red Grande Homes logo across, where the words are set out to make the shape of a cat. Apparently cats symbolise *new but stylish homes, the cosy and the sleek.* I heard Greg Martin say those exact words. Greg Martin is the person in charge of all the salespeople who work from the show home. It's their job to get people to sign up to buy other houses on the estate, and his job to be in charge of them doing that. He seems to be very good at it because the show home is really busy and when people step out of it they have often signed up to buy a house, looking about them with dazed-but-excited expressions on their faces. Little do they know.

"How much would it cost if I bought all the same stuff that you've got in here?" a man in a suit and raincoat asks him, as I listen in while pretending not to.

"Well, we actually have catalogue links to all the products, and there's an option to buy fully decorated and furnished," says Greg Martin. "It works out over ten thousand pounds cheaper than if you bought all the items separately."

The man looks impressed and they both go inside. I notice he didn't actually answer the man's question about how much it would cost and I imagine Greg Martin gets people to buy houses on the South Downs Estate by doing that swirly-eyed hypnotising thing they always have in cartoons.

"*You will buy a house on the South Downs Estate. You will move all your family away from the people they like, and the woodland they run in, and all the bits and pieces that have made their life what it is so far, and join the many robot humans in our roll-out plastic house city.*"

That's what our new street reminds me of. Those roll-out play mats toddlers have. *Here is a road. Here is a house. Here is a zebra crossing.* Who knows what's underneath all the concrete? Whole worlds made flat and forgotten. Maybe they could roll me out a bunch of new friends while they're at it. I know that's not how it works, but it would be great if it was.

We're one of the last families to move into Ridgeway Close. Some of the gardens look so perfect I can't imagine anyone actually playing in them. Dad said there was some sort of contract that meant you could get a reduced price on your deposit to buy, if you kept your garden in a certain manner for the length of time the show home was on the street. And there's a fine if you let it overgrow. It's our job to give a good impression to potential buyers. It's like living inside an advert on TV.

"What happens if you want to make your garden be full of toilets with stuff growing in them or something?"

"Why would anyone want to do that?" said Dad, looking confused.

"It was just an example."

In the margin of my notebook I make a list of all the house numbers in our little bit of the close. 10, 12, 14, 16, 18, 20, 22, 24, then the four flats, 11, 13, 15 and 17. And us at number 16. So far I've worked out that two couples live in the top flats, 15 and 17, who are friends, because I saw them out on their little balcony in the evening drinking wine and smoking cigarettes and getting louder in how they laugh. Dad said the women were "proper beauties", which I thought was embarrassing and made me cringe.

Mum and Dad don't often say that sort of thing to each other. In the mobile home I used to catch Mum sometimes, flipping through old photograph books of when they were younger, before me and Lolly were born, and sighing.

"What's wrong?" I asked.

"Everything," she said, and I worried then because everything is a lot of things, so I went into the kitchen and made her a cheese, cucumber and salad cream sandwich and put it next to two homemade (by me) ginger biscuits on a plate, poured her a cup of milk, and put some daisy heads floating in a glass of water for decoration. It looked pretty and I took the whole lot in to her on a tray.

Mum looked at me, and I thought she was going to cry. "That's so thoughtful, Luna," she said.

"Do you feel better?"

"Yes. Much. I know I get very sad sometimes. But I hope you know it's not because of you."

I like making food for people because it usually

makes them feel better. It's easy with Lolly. She likes anything that's cut into star shapes, which is easier with some foods than others.

It's then I realise my brain is wandering, and I'm not really being a very good detective because I didn't even notice the boy, with the backpack and the long hair with the headband on, come and sit next to me on the kerb.

"Hello," says the boy with the backpack and the long hair and the headband on, sitting next to me on the kerb.

"Hello," I say.

"You're in number sixteen, aren't you?"

"Yes."

"I'm in number twenty-two. Right opposite. I'm Rudo."

"I'm Luna," I say. "Do you like baking?" I have no idea why I ask this because I know it's good to start conversations with something less specific.

"Not really," said Rudo easily. "I like *eating*, though."

This, I think, is what my dad would call a *match made in heaven*.

"Can I show you something really brilliant?" he says.

I don't know what makes me say yes. I was quite happy sitting on the shiny new kerb making my list of any interesting or suspicious activity, totally and utterly by myself. But Rudo smiles at me, stands up and starts walking away, turning to see if I'm going with him, and, for whatever reason, I get up and follow him.

CHAPTER
2

I follow Rudo all along the back fence of the show home. He seems quite relaxed about it as he pulls over one of the recycling tubs, then stands on it, and starts pulling himself over the fence using the tub to bunk himself over.

"We're not doing anything *illegal*, are we?" I say. The last thing I need is to get into that sort of trouble on the day before I start my new school, and Mum and Dad really don't need the stress. But Rudo turns round and gives me a grin, the sort that says, "Maybe, but there's a loophole, and everything will be fine." So I continue as though this is the case. I can always point at him if we get in trouble. I can always say, "He told me to do it!" But, I wouldn't do that. Experience shows I'd be more likely to take the blame, annoyingly.

Soon he is up and over, and I can feel my heart beating fast in my chest, because I've got one of my legs over the top of the fence too, while the other foot is on tiptoes on top of the recycling tub. I pull myself over, which is harder than it looks because the fence is actually quite thin and a bit wobbly, and land with a soft thump, right next to him, on some soft but very neat grass. We are in a back garden. Not just any back garden, *but the back garden of dreams.*

"Should I be regretting this?" I say.

"No!" he says, smiling, pulling me down to the ground, so we're hiding behind a water feature in the shape of a beehive.

"Isn't there CCTV?" I look about for little cameras, or those red laser beams you see in movies when art thieves are trying to steal the *Mona Lisa.*

"There is," he says slowly, "but not on this bit of the garden because they forgot, with all the focus on *there.*" He nods at the house, which even on the outside is the cleanest and neatest house that has ever existed. The Grande Homes Show Home. *The home of homes.* The shadows of the two big flagpoles loom over the garden like two guards, and even though I'm acting like I'm OK about all this, like *it's no big deal to me actually*, I'm worried about getting into trouble. "And we can *sneak*," he says, laughing to himself as he starts crawling along the grass, stopping to lay flat behind glazed plant pots, in an over-dramatic way. The way he moves makes me laugh too.

"I'm good at sneaking," he says proudly. "It's my specialist skill." He sounds half proud and half sad about that.

The garden is the *perfect garden*: flowers, pond, the water feature, a lovely set of tables and chairs, statues, and even a vegetable garden. I feel a sort of swoop in my chest, the memory of home, but as I reach over to touch the spray of carrot leaves, as we crawl past, it turns out they're *plastic.* Who would go to all the trouble of setting up a beautiful garden that was *full of fake vegetables*? I feel like I'm in a sci-fi movie, one with a scary plot where everybody turns into robots and there's only me and Lolly left who are human or something. But I keep crawling after Rudo anyway. He certainly doesn't move like a robot.

As it turns out, it's not the actual garden he's interested in. Soon he's crawling round the base of the big pear tree, the one they must have kept from when this was moorland, before they cleared it to start again, because it's thick and has branches like it's been reaching upwards for a very long time. He gets to a rope ladder at the back of the tree, turns to me and nods enthusiastically.

I already like that about him, that he's not afraid to be excited. Some people pretend to not be excited about anything. They are not the sort of people who could ever be my friend. Not that I have much experience of friends, but that's something about people I've noticed by being a detective.

"Look at Luna Loveridge *staring* at everyone!" is what Penny Robinson used to say, and people would laugh. But I wasn't staring. I was *watching*. There's a difference.

I look up. There, in the branches, is the absolute biggest and swankiest tree house I've ever seen. Somebody could live in it *and* have some servants (even though I don't believe in having servants) living in it too – it's that big. And it has been made to look like a proper house, like a miniature version in the same style as the real ones on Ridgeway Close.

"Actual wow," I say with my mouth open.

"Come on then," he says, beckoning me over, as he starts to climb the ladder, hidden from the windows of the house. "Sometimes it's worth sneaking."

For some reason, once again I follow.

But, oh! Inside is just wonderful!

The whole place is set out like a one-room version of my own house, and I guess most of the others on Ridgeway Close. There's a kid-size sofa, slate grey, with mustard cushions, and two armchairs, two orange beanbags, and a stripy rug to show where the living-room area is. Then there's a glass dining table – you can tell nobody is going to use it, who'd put a glass dining table in an area just for kids? – and some metal chairs, the sort that look nice but which fall apart after a month of people actually using them, but still. There's a shelf with loads of board games stacked, and a socket board, with loads of different holes for plugs and chargers, and two USB ports. There is an old-fashioned TV, a big square one, and I'm looking at the fake kitchen, wondering if it *is* actually fake... There's a three-quarter-size electric cooker, with hob, and if it works, *if it works, I'm coming here all the time and never leaving.*

"So," says Rudo, looking proud of himself, "this is the clubhouse."

"The clubhouse," I say slowly. "What club?"

"It hasn't got a name yet," he says with a shrug.

"But that's a minor detail."

"How many members?"

"One." He looks at me. "Potentially two…"

"Are you inviting me to join your club?"

"It's a possibility."

I laugh, feeling brave. Something about Rudo makes me feel brave. "I'm not committing to something before I know what it is. Would we be in big trouble if we got found in here?"

"What do you think?" he says, making himself comfortable on a big orange beanbag. He really looks at home here. "And there aren't any rules in this club. Not really."

"What I'm asking is, wouldn't we be in *huge* amounts of trouble if we got found in here? Couldn't they throw us out of our *actual* houses?"

"Ah, nahhh. Our families own them, even if they are on one hundred per cent mortgages that they'll have to pay back every month, possibly for the rest of their lives," he says, "so I think it's unlikely we'd get more than a bit of a lecture and told not to do it again. Maybe have to write a letter to someone saying sorry. Maybe have *Greg Martin* take us by our ears to our parents, like in a movie or something, and our parents grounding us…?"

"Yeah, maybe," I say. "And I don't think my parents would ever ground me."

"Neither would my mum," says Rudo quickly. "And *I'm* not afraid of Greg Martin."

"And neither am I," I say even quicker. Truth is, I *am* a bit afraid of Greg Martin, not because he might tell me off, but because of the way his face changes in the gaps between when he's talking to potential customers. That smile, that huge smile, which drops to nothing when nobody who's going to buy something from him is looking. Except me.

"And the club," says Rudo, "is any kid we like and decide to tell about it, but we have to check with the other first."

"How are we going to decide who we tell about it?"

Rudo shrugs and opens a cupboard in the kitchen, bringing out a packet of chocolate digestives and some sachets of hot chocolate like they have in hotel rooms.

"You're the first I've told," he says, flicking on a real kettle. "We can work out who to tell next. At some point."

"Why did you choose me?"

"You were spying on people," he says.

"I wasn't!" I say quickly.

"Come off it," he says. "I saw you when *I* was spying on *you*. It's fine. It's why I knew we'd get on."

"I'm not sure how I feel about having someone spy on *me* while *I* spy on other people." This makes us both laugh, and I feel sort of happy. "They have a working kettle in here?" I say, trying not to feel too excited about the fact Rudo has chosen me, first, to come to the clubhouse.

"I brought that," he says proudly. "I brought lots of things. They don't check in the cupboards. Nobody really comes up here. Not often enough to really *notice* anything anyway. Something *I've* noticed is that people very often come and look at houses they're going to move into, *without* their kids. It's like a conspiracy."

That makes no sense to me. If I had children, the first thing I'd be looking at was the inside of this tree house. And I'd be bringing them with me to look. But Rudo is right. Mum and Dad came to view number 16 without me and Lolly. And by the time we *did* see it, it was all decided.

"It's amazing," I say again. "Thank you for bringing me."

"Ah, no problem," says Rudo with a shrug, pouring hot water into two mustard-striped mugs. "I didn't even ask if you want one. How rude. Do you?"

"I pretty much always want hot chocolate," I say, truthfully.

We take our drinks over to the sofa, sit, and each wrap our hands lightly round our mugs, blowing on the steam without saying anything. You can see the diggers and cranes working on the other streets through one window and the other side of Ridgeway Close through the other. You could probably really spy on people from here. If you wanted to.

"So what sort of things do you like?" I say, after a mouthful of hot chocolate. It's sort of thin and lumpy, like it's come from a machine, because Rudo didn't stir it, but it still tastes good. "Other than breaking into tree houses, that is?"

Rudo smiles. "Ha! I like space stuff, planets. And I like drawing, drawing people's hands and eyes and their hair. Little portraits. And dancing. I go to tap lessons." He gives me a side look. "I like old movies, with dancing in." He pauses as if waiting for laughter, which certainly won't be coming from me. I love old movies too. "I like … um … murals. You know. Big pictures on the sides of buildings and public places … like big, bright messages to people as they go past… What about you?"

"Baking," I say immediately. "I can bake most things. Huge cakes, buns, pastries full of sweet custard. I like notebooks. Making notes. I like detective stories and my little sister, Lolly. You'll meet her. She's funny and smells of candyfloss. I have no idea why, but she does. I love the smell of clean laundry. And my mum's perfume; she gets posh stuff from a big shop in London once a year, it's got orange oil in it. And, I like it really early in the morning when nobody else is awake. That's my favourite time of day."

"Maybe sometimes," says Rudo, looking thoughtful, "at that time of day, you could sneak out and come here. I do sometimes."

"Don't your mum or dad mind?" I remember not everyone lives with their mum and dad and want to ask the question better. "Or whoever you live with…?"

But Rudo shrugs, and I don't push it.

"Fancy a game of cards?" he says, pulling a pack from the shelf with the other board games. "Do you know how to play rummy?"

CHAPTER
3

When I've beaten Rudo at three hands of cards and taught him how to play rummy properly, not the small-kid version, and we've had some chewy strawberry sweets from his backpack and eaten most of the chocolate digestives, he gets up and goes over to the little sink, pours some water out of a plastic tap, and starts washing up our cups.

"How is there water in here?" I say. They can't have plumbed it in. Even I know that would be expensive and sort of impossible.

"There's a tank, see?" he says, pointing at a big flask thing attached under the sink. "We just have to remember to fill it up. And it won't be hot water. Unless you boil it."

"How long have you been coming in here?"

Rudo shrugs. "Long enough. Right. I've got to get home," he says suddenly. "What about you? You coming now, or going to stay?"

I think carefully about this. I'd actually quite like to stay, alone in the secret clubhouse, lie down on the sofa and just sort of, *be*, for a while. But also, I will need a bath and all those things you need to do the day before you start a new school. Plus Dad will worry. And Mum.

"I'm going too," I decide. "Is it OK if I come

back here, even when you're not... I mean, I'd like to come with you again..." For some reason I'm not being guarded at all with Rudo. It usually takes ages for me to speak to someone, after I've made sure they're not tricking me, or trying to steal something from me, or they're not going to prank me and tell everyone else all about how gullible I am.

"Of course," says Rudo, putting his backpack over his shoulders. "And until we ask some others, this is ours now. So use it how you like. I'm definitely not in charge." He makes his way to the door. "I don't agree with people being in charge. If someone's in charge, that means someone's not in charge, and that's not fair, is it?"

I'd never thought of it that way before.

When he's climbed out, and I've climbed out, we make our way down the ladder at the back of the tree, and there's that fear of being caught again that makes my heart loud, but we crawl across the garden, keeping ourselves hidden behind things, and then we are over the fence, each of us in turn, back on the recycling tub, and on to the pavement as though none of it had happened.

"Today was a risk really," says Rudo, looking sheepish. "I usually only go in there after dark or early in the morning, when the house itself is shut. But sometimes it's worth it."

"*Now* he tells me," I laugh, but I'm not cross. "Thank you for taking me," I say. "I love it."

"Sometimes it's nice to hang out with your friends with no grown-ups around," he says, and I nod enthusiastically in agreement. Plus I'm beaming at the word *friends*.

"Too right," I say overconfidently. I've not really had proper friends before, so I have nothing to compare it to. But today was ace.

"Right. Catch you later," he says. "Better get back for tea."

"Me too. See you soon!" I wave, but he's already off, walking with a sort of a bounce, like there are springs in the bottom of his trainers. I didn't even ask him how old he is, or where he goes to school. *Dear universe, please let him go to South Downs Junior School, and let us be friends, and let moving to Ridgeway Close be a good thing, and let all of us be happy.*

PS Failing that, just a few nice days would do, thank you.

At the new house the car is in the drive and the front door is unlocked so I push down the handle and go inside.

There are still things in boxes because we haven't finishing unpacking. The living room has the new sofa Mum and Dad ordered through Grande Homes, which is made to fit perfectly, slate grey with mustard-yellow cushions – like the one in the tree house, just bigger. It's still got the plastic covering on. We need some photos up on the walls. We need the ornaments unpacked. We need to at least try to make it look like home. At the moment it smells so new it actually makes me feel like I'm going to be sick.

I walk into the kitchen, which is the one place downstairs that *is* totally unpacked and set up properly. It was the first thing we all did. All the pans are hanging from those big hooks over the sink, and the jug with the utensils in is sitting on the counter, and the cutlery is set out neatly in the right drawer. There are spotty mugs on the mug tree, and the fridge-freezer is humming quietly, like fridge-freezers do, like they are thinking about all the important things in the universe at once. That's why you sometimes hear them cracking.

"Hello!" I shout up the stairs. "Anyone home?"

There's no answer.

New houses are strange. They smell odd, and they feel odd, like you can still see the brushstrokes on the paintwork, and the thumb prints of the builders on the kitchen counter, and the idea someone else had about what will happen in that house, and none of it, not one bit of it, has anything to do with how whoever moves in will use it, or what *will* happen.

I go up the stairs. I can hear the TV on in my parents' bedroom.

When I push the door open, the first thing I see is my dad, lying on his back on the bed, his eyes closed, and his chest going up and down in that over-exaggerated way people's bodies move when they're asleep. He must be tired. Moving house *is* tiring. He's snoring a bit. Those deep breaths that sound like old machinery. On the bedside table is a plate with some crusts of oven pizza left on it and three empty beer cans, crushed into flat misshapes, ready for recycling.

The next thing I see is Lolly. She's curled up at the bottom of the bed under a blanket, holding

Giraffey, the soft toy she's had with her since she was a baby. For a minute she looks much younger than six, like a toddler, all bundled up and cuddly. She's still in her day clothes but is fast asleep too. I wonder whether I should wake her up, make sure she's had something to eat, and is clean, ready for tomorrow. Mum's new job in the twenty-four-hour garage as a supervisor means she won't be in until late. I don't want her to know Dad has been drinking beer and fallen asleep when he's on Lolly duty. I don't want them to argue about it.

Also, he'd said he wouldn't drink beer when we moved house.

I decide not to wake anyone up, but because I don't want Lolly to get squashed in the night by Dad, or by Mum when she gets in, what I do is, I go into her bedroom, and get her bed ready, put the nightlight on, pull back the duvet, then I go to Mum and Dad's room, lift her up, very gently so as not to wake her, then carry her through to her bed.

I tuck her in, put Giraffey next to her, and watch her for a bit. Her new uniform is still in the plastic packets from the supermarket, piled up on the side, so I open the white T-shirts with the collar, and the leggings, and I hang them over the back of her door handle. There are new pants, with dogs on, and new socks too, but I leave them in the packets so she can choose whichever ones she wants to wear tomorrow. I hope Mum will be pleased that I'm being helpful. I can always pretend Dad did it. Then she can be pleased with him instead.

When I've set out my own uniform in my own room, I go back downstairs. It's getting late, past nine o'clock, but I still haven't had my tea. Cheese on toast will do, so I grate the cheese, put it on the bread under the grill, wait for the cheese to bubble and turn brown at the edges, then put it on a plate with a big blob of ketchup. I sit eating it on the sofa watching a detective drama on the TV, one about a detective who goes undercover in a school, and I think about how I could pretend I was an undercover detective tomorrow and become a hero when I discover some secret plot that's been going on under everyone's noses, and have my photo in the paper under the headline, NEW GIRL SAVES THE DAY.

When I'm finished, I rinse the plate under the hot tap rather than stack it in the shiny new dishwasher. I am suspicious of it. I want to know where all the dirt goes. Outside it's dark now. I lock the front door and hang the key on the hook. (Mum should have the other key for when she gets home.) I close all the curtains. I leave the light on in the porch.

In my room I get my phone, which was Dad's old, old one, but still does all the things I want it to do, out of my drawer and send Mum a message. I hope it will make her smile.

Night-night, Mum, I type. I ♥ you very much. C u when you get home xxxx

It's annoying because it doesn't show that it's delivered. There must be something wrong with Mum's phone. I turn off the bedroom light and go to look out of the window. If the light is on, people will see me, and I can't be nosy if people can see me, so I stand in the dark, at the window, looking out over Ridgeway Close. From my bedroom window I can see the front of Rudo's house. There are lights on upstairs, and if the layout of his house is the same as ours, the one on the left must be his bedroom.

That's when I see two things that I have to write down in my notebook.

The first is the silhouette of a woman in the upstairs window of number 12, the big posh house on the corner, the biggest of all the houses on Ridgeway Close. She looks like she's sawing something, chopping something up, and I try not to let my imagination run away with me. I write down the time next to a description of what it looks like she's doing.

The second is somebody the same size and shape as Rudo, with the same long hair pushed back with a headband, coming out of his front door and gently closing it behind them. In the street lamp I can see that, whoever it is, they've got a backpack with them. They're carrying a torch, and have the collar of their coat pushed up, as though they're trying to hide their face. I think they look up towards my window, and I duck down quickly. I hope they haven't seen me spying on them. If it *is* Rudo, I hope he's OK. But, I just can't think of a reason for a ten-year-old boy to be sneaking out of his house at night. *Maybe he sleeps in the clubhouse sometimes?* The thought of that is sort of exciting.

I try to stay awake so that I can give Mum a cuddle when she gets in from her shift, but it's no good, I'm really sleepy, and before I know it, I'm drifting off into a dream where I'm baking a big cake in the shape of a tree house, and Rudo is there, eating the red icing from the roof with a big silver spoon he's pulled from his backpack.

CHAPTER
4

I can't believe I overslept and missed Mum before she'd gone back into work.

Her new boss is being totally unfair, making her do a late shift and then an early one, on her first day of work when we've just moved in, but I suppose, because Dad's off, it's OK really. It's not like we've been *abandoned*. I feel selfish that I want her to be here when she's got so much to do, so I tell Lolly that Mum's left us homemade pancakes for breakfast with little faces made out of blueberries and raspberries, and we eat them at the table while Dad has a shower. I don't need to tell her I made them. Mum would have made them if she'd had time, I know it.

When Dad comes downstairs he's wearing the same outfit that he fell asleep in yesterday, and I think he should do some laundry instead of waiting for Mum to do it, because Mum is at work, and who says the woman has to do it anyway? That annoys me. They both have jobs and he's got over two more weeks off. Why should it be Mum? Dad's mum, Gran, always says, "Is she not looking after you properly, Warren?" and I get cross about it because a) Dad is a grown-up and b) Mum is not his parent, so who said she has to look after him anyway? How about he look after her? How about they take it in turns? How about *that*?

Anyway, Lolly is excited and can't stop talking.

"So there's this boy in my class, Jax, and he can put the tip of his tongue in his nostril, like, stick it right up, and I'm going to practise until I can do it too." She is sticking her tongue up her nose, trying to anyway, pulling silly faces as she twists and turns her tongue, which is nowhere near long enough. "I showed him how I can roll my tongue into three," she says, grinning as Dad is suddenly bundling us out of the house and into the car, leaving the dirty breakfast things on the table, before we've even had a chance to clean our teeth. He's lucky I got us both ready. "*And* I beat him at thumb wars. Is Mummy picking us up?" she says to Dad suddenly as I click her seat belt in and then mine.

Dad pulls the car away and off down Ridgeway Close. "I've booked you both in on the bus for the usual days," he says, checking his wing mirror. "I thought it would be a good way to meet other kids from your class, and the street. I know there's a girl from your school in number twelve. I was talking to her mum. Your bus passes should be at reception at your school, Luna. All you need to do is go in and pick them up. The teachers will tell you where to go to catch it. There's quite a few of you, apparently."

Number 12. I think of the woman sawing in the middle of the night and shiver. It hadn't crossed my mind that a child might live there too.

Dad nods at the bus stop on the corner as we pass. There are a group of kids in the same uniforms as us, standing about, holding their phones, leaning on each other, laughing. I look out for Rudo, but he's not with them. He must go to another school. Or not have come home last night, if that was him leaving his house. I am suddenly, on top of everything else, worried about him. I promise myself I'll find time to go to the clubhouse after school without giving the game away to Lolly. Somehow.

Dad drives us to the main gates and goes to hand us our lunch when we all realise we left our lunchboxes on the kitchen table. So he rummages his hand in his pockets for change, but he only has fifty-seven pence, so he says he'll call the office and explain and pay them back tomorrow.

I don't remind him that they have thumbprint technology and we are supposed to pay online, and then that gets added to the account, and that it was all set up the day we first visited. Or that I stuck the password to the new fridge-freezer with a magnet so he'd remember, because he looks like he might not be able to handle this piece of information today.

What I hope is he'll go home and have a bath and start showing us that this great moving-house idea of his is actually for the best, and not the worst idea in the world. He's not really doing a great job of that so far, and Mum is almost invisible.

As Dad drives away, Lolly squeezes my hand and I squeeze hers back. All around us are new kids, in different uniforms than we are used to, and I feel like I might cry, but I don't, not because there's anything wrong with crying, but because I don't want to scare Lolly. And because if I start, I might think of all the things I miss about before, and I might never, ever stop.

We walk through the crowds towards the infant school, because it's next to mine, just a short path to walk between the two of us. We walk together and Lolly's holding my hand, and she looks super smart and cute in her new uniform, which has a purple jumper and white collared T-shirt, and the leggings she chose to go with it, and Mum said that was fine because it meant she could jump about more, and if anybody says anything, she'll write a note. I like that about Mum. She lets us be ourselves.

"They've got a sandpit," says Lolly. "And a water area. And at lunch, if it's sunny, you can eat your packed lunch on the school field." She frowns. "Not today, though, because we forgot our lunch."

"Dad will ring the school," I say, trying to sound convincing.

Because I'm the best in the house at making food, I offered to do Lolly's lunch. I'd made her favourite, chicken and tomato and pickle sandwiches, a smoothie, an apple, and one of the flapjacks I brought with us from the old house. The list of things that are allowed and not allowed in packed lunches at South Downs Infants School is spelled out in great detail, and it said no cakes, but flapjacks aren't cakes and these ones are homemade, which has to count for something.

It's a shame it's sitting neatly on the kitchen table. I'll set two alarms tomorrow.

I give Lolly a note I've written but signed as if it's from Mum. If I was Lolly, I'd want a note from Mum, and if I was Mum, I'd want me to do it for her because she is so busy at work and would be upset that she hasn't had time to do the things for Lolly she'd like to. It's not *really* lying. It's making things the way they should be.

"Mum left this to give to you before she went to work this morning," I say. Lolly smiles and grabs at the piece of paper. She reads it herself, out loud, in that slow reading voice little kids do.

"*To Lolly, have a lovely first day at your new school. I ♥ you so much. Kisses and cuddles, Mummy xxxxx*"

She smiles and clutches the note tightly between her fingers and I know I was right to write it. I'm pretty good at doing Mum's writing now.

"Hello, Lolly!" says her class teacher, smiling from the doorway, waving her hand to greet her. Miss Zhao has a lovely smile and is wearing a dress with a marshmallow pattern on.

"Hello, Miss Zhao!" says Lolly.

"I'll be walking over to pick her up," I say,

and Miss Zhao smiles. I lean forward as Lolly is hanging up her coat. "My dad left the lunch on the table, and she'll need a hot dinner today. She'll be packed lunches normally."

"Thank you for letting me know. I'll make sure we sort something. It's such a lot to remember, moving house and changing schools." She gives me a look I can't interpret. "You have a lovely day at your new school, Luna, won't you?"

"Yes," I say. "Have a lovely day too, Miss Zhao. And you, Lolly!" When I'm sure Lolly's safely inside, and happy about it, I walk away, carefully and slowly, until I'm inside the door of my new school, holding my bag, my heart beating so loudly it's all I can hear. I wonder if anyone else can hear it.

I haven't met Mrs Locke since when we visited last year. She's different than I remember. She's stopped dying her hair and it's in a big white quiff and she's wearing a stud in her nose that sparkles purple as she greets me at the door. And she's smiling. She looks kind, and I nearly burst into tears again.

"My dad forgot our lunch," I say quickly. "He didn't mean to. And I need to pick up mine and

Lolly's bus passes."

"Hello, Luna!" says Mrs Locke. "No problem. We'll sort something. There's a lot to remember on the first day. Come in and hang everything up. Then I can introduce you."

I do what she says. There's a peg with someone else's name on it, *Zoe*, which has been crossed out, and my name, *Luna*, has been written above it in black marker. I'd have liked a brand-new sticker if I'm honest, but at least I have a peg of my own. I look at the other kids hanging up their stuff. The hallway is a blur of faces and I wonder if I could possibly be happy here. It smells just the same as my old school. Something cooking, from down the corridor, cleaning fluid, poster paint. Someone's sprayed an aerosol deodorant, somewhere.

"In you come, Luna," says Mrs Locke. I like her stripy trousers; she reminds me of a pirate. "Let me introduce you to everyone and get you seated at your table. Have you got a book? Choose one from the shelf at the front, if not. We *love* reading at South Downs Junior School!" She says it in a way that makes me wonder if that's true.

I choose a book from the box at the front, one

with a boy and girl playing football on it, and then there's a bustle while everyone comes in, pencil cases are brought out, and everyone gets out a book and starts reading. I look at the timetable on the wall, which says *SILENT READING, MATHS, LITERACY, BREAK, MATHS, LUNCH, SPELLINGS, PE, TOPIC*. There are illustrations on the cards to go with each lesson that someone has done, and they are brilliant. Fine details of people, big swoops of hair and funny faces.

"Everyone, this is Luna," says Mrs Locke when the rest of the class has settled. "She's with us for the rest of Year Six and will be going to the high school with you in September. Please make her feel welcome." She directs me to a table that has a spare seat at it, and I slide into it and put my book and pencil case down in front of me.

"Hello, Luna," say the rest of the class, and I manage a small, yet firm, "Hi."

I smile at the girl sitting opposite me, who has a heart-shaped sticker saying *Jennifer Browne* on her pencil case, and she raises an eyebrow at me and looks towards the boy sitting next to her. They both sort of shrug. Not a good start.

"The first thing I want to announce," says Mrs

Locke, "is that we are running the Great Big Family Baking Competition again this term after the success of last year, and we'd like as many pupils as possible to make up duos with adults in their lives and enter."

I jolt. *The Great Big Family Baking Competition.* That sounds exactly like something I need to get involved with. Right now.

"Is there anyone who's interested?" says Mrs Locke. "You can have one of the flyers with all the details. Deadline for entry is the end of this week…"

"Me!" I say loudly without putting my hand up. "Me! I want to enter. Me and my mum!"

Somebody behind me sniggers but I don't care. Mrs Locke smiles and passes me a flyer, and there, in my hand and printed on bright orange paper, is the answer to everything.

CHAPTER 5

South Downs Junior School presents:
THE GREAT BIG FAMILY BAKING COMPETITION

One pupil. One family member. (By family we mean parent, or guardian, or carer, or grandparent … or any other adult who is involved in your care or family life.) One amazing platter or showstopper of cakes or breads or pasties with the theme Under the Sea.

The main components of the baking will be done at home, but decoration and final assembly will take place in the school hall.

All entrance forms to be in by this Friday at the very latest for acceptance into the competition next Friday.

Prize: £100 in shopping vouchers, day out in London, including travel and dinner, plus tickets for four people to enjoy a West End show of the winner's choice.

I'm already filling out the form.
I have to win. I *have to* win. This is exactly what

we need. The four of us, out for a lovely day in London together. And me and Mum, planning what we'll make, practising in the kitchen, laughing. I imagine us with icing on our faces and her flicking some at me with a wooden spoon, and the radio on, and Lolly taste-testing everything. Like we used to.

Jennifer Browne puts her hand up too. "I'd like a flyer, Mrs Locke! My mum is a professional and runs her own restaurant, *as you know*. Does that mean we can't do it together? Will she be *disqualified*?" She says the last word with great emphasis. "Will she be *too good*?"

"I don't think that will be a problem," says Mrs Locke. "All welcome, of course. I think this would be a good thing to balance out all that hard work you're doing in the lead up to your SATs."

"Good point, Mrs Locke!" says Jennifer Browne brightly. Then she turns towards me. "What does *your* mum do?" Jennifer Browne says, addressing me directly.

"Do for what?" I say. She does lots of things. She makes amazing meals. She can do her hair like someone from the 1950s. She makes me laugh. She reads books, all sorts of them, with men and women standing on beaches and on windswept islands and on cobbled streets on the shiny covers. She always has one next to the bed beside a new nail polish. She smokes cigarettes that are rolled in dark brown paper, never in the house, and always leaves a ring of lipstick round them. She makes swans out of napkins at birthday parties, and little statues out of old silver foil and lines them up on the kitchen windowsill. She has painted fingernails and painted toenails, never the same colour. She wears flipflops in the house, even in winter, and you can hear her walking about in the other room, the familiar flap of plastic against her size-seven feet. She goes swimming in the sea, and in lakes, and lots of places you're not supposed to, and she lets us do it with her. She has a different voice when she's using the phone. She is kind and silly and sometimes grumpy or sad, but she always tells me it isn't my fault. For my last birthday, she made me a cake in the shape of Doctor Who's TARDIS, and the icing tasted of peppermint. She's my brilliant mum.

I realise Jennifer Browne is still talking to me.

"For a job. For *mo-ney*," she says, slowly and

loudly, as if that should have been obvious in the first place. I realise I still haven't answered.

"She works in the twenty-four-hour garage," I say, wishing immediately I hadn't, because Jennifer pulls a face as though I've said the most unintentionally funny thing since time began.

"Ha! I suppose heating up pastries in a microwave counts as baking to *some* people." She laughs loudly and so does the boy next to her.

I screw my face up and try to think of something to say in return. I should have known there'd be a Penny Robinson Mark Two at South Downs Juniors. There's one at every school. More than one. And they *always* seem to find a way to get at me. So, yes, it's my first day, my first lesson, and I've already got that feeling you get when someone humiliates you and you feel like shouting and crying and your skin is as hot as the back seat of the car on a day at the beach. I'm about to say something clever in response, although I don't know what. And I'm also excited about the baking competition, because I know it doesn't really matter what Jennifer Browne says – I know my mum and me are great bakers, *and we can win this.*

"I'd like a flyer please, Mrs Locke," says another girl on another table. She turns to me and smiles. "My mum works at the supermarket in town. She's on the meat counter."

Jennifer Browne mimes being sick.

"Although I'm a vegetarian," adds the girl, and then turns to me. "I'm Meg. Pleased to meet you."

"Pleased to meet you too," I say, and smile back.

I hear Jennifer Browne tut loudly behind me.

Before I think of something to say the door opens and in stumbles a late student saying, "Sorry, Mrs Locke, there was a family emergency." And I look up, and there, with his long hair and his headband and his backpack and his hands in his pockets, is Rudo.

I can't believe it! The universe, for once, has delivered! Doubly delivered because Rudo walks straight over and sits in the space right next to me at the table and unpacks his school diary and his pencil case.

"Late again, Rudo*lph*," says Jennifer Browne, leaning over the table and tapping at his pencil case. "Tut, tut, tut. Maybe the new girl can get her mum to heat up some sausage rolls at the twenty-four-hour garage to keep your energy up. You're always so tired these days!"

Rudo doesn't reply, rolls his eyes instead, and pushes his hairband back so his hair is totally away from his face. He turns and smiles at me.

"Hello, Luna, who likes baking and when-it's-very-early-in-the-morning," he whispers.

"Hello, Rudo, who likes space and tap-dancing and pictures on buildings," I say, and laugh. "I can't believe we're in the same class!"

"We are," he smiles. "A nice twist of fate, right?"

I am relieved he's pleased to see me. I didn't want him to be one of those *I'll be your friend outside of school but don't you dare talk to me at school* kind of friends. I had some of them where I used to live, and it always made me feel awful. One day I'll have a friend who's so proud to be my friend they'll march down the high street bashing cymbals together saying, "Luna Rae Loveridge is my friend and I think she's wonderful."

Imagine someone liking you that much. Just because you're you.

"You OK, by the way?" I think of what I saw last night, the person creeping out of Rudo's house at half past nine, with the backpack and torch. I would probably be afraid to be out in the dark at night like that by myself.

"Yes. All good," he says, not altogether convincingly. "You?"

"Yes," I say quickly. "I want to talk to you about the woman who lives in the posh house on the corner. Number twelve."

Rudo raises his eyebrows and pulls a face. "Oh good," he says. "Because I wanted to talk to you about…"

"Greg Martin," we both whisper at the same time.

We look at each other and grin.

"I guess our club is going to be really nosy then," he says.

"I guess so."

"We'd better find some other members. Fancy scouting for some later?"

"For definite," I say. Although I don't really. I quite fancy it being a club of two.

"Maybe I could come round yours after school?" whispers Rudo when Mrs Locke isn't looking and I gulp at the thought of him standing in our living room, with the cellophane-wrapped sofa and everything not quite unpacked, unless Dad has done it while Mum is at work. I'm about to say, "No, that's not a good idea, maybe I can come round yours?" when Jennifer Browne puts her hand up and says, "Mrs Locke, Rudo and the new girl are putting me off my reading. We all know how important our SATs year is."

Rudo rolls his eyes and she sticks her tongue out at him.

"While it's lovely you're being so welcoming to our new class member," says Mrs Locke in a serious voice, "we're supposed to be focusing on our *silent* reading for our quizzes later *to check for understanding*, which, by the very name of the activity, needs to be done *in silence*."

"Sorry, Mrs Locke," we both say, pulling our books nearer to us and leaning over them as though we are paying them any attention whatsoever.

"I don't think mine is quite sorted yet, though. The house and the furniture. Maybe I can come round yours?" I whisper.

Rudo's eyes widen and he shakes his head

immediately. "Not a good idea. We've got … stuff … going on at ours at the moment. The tree house, though. We should just meet there."

I think, yes, I will be there – and Dad, or Mum, or anyone can put Lolly to bed because they both said it would be good for me to make new friends when we moved, and that's exactly what I'm doing.

"What time?" I ask.

Mrs Locke comes over to our table, stealthy as a ninja, and I jump.

"Jennifer has a point, you two," she says seriously. "Take this as a warning, otherwise I'll have to separate you." She's smiling, though, like she knows I've made a friend and how important that is to me, and I'm glad, because the last thing I need right now is an unfair teacher. I go back to pretending to read my book but really I'm thinking about what we might make for the Great Big Family Baking Competition, and iced layer cakes decorated with big swirls of icing and bright purple cherries. In my head, Mum and I have got the radio on, and we're using a spatula and a turntable to make the first lot of icing very smooth.

"Clubhouse tonight," Rudo whispers, and I nod.

I can't wait. I'll definitely be there. And I can't wait to plan mine and Mum's entry in the baking competition because it's *exactly* what my family needs right now. I look up and see Jennifer Browne staring at me, just sitting there staring, so I stare right back until she looks away. I'm not going to let *anyone* get in my way, especially not Jennifer Browne and her restaurant-owning mum. If she thinks I'm going to give up that easily, she has no idea who she's dealing with

CHAPTER
6

At the end of the day there is a misunderstanding about bus passes, because Dad has filled in the wrong form, or sent it to the wrong place or something like that, so I stand with Lolly, watching the school bus drive off, with Rudo and any other kids from Ridgeway Close who I was hoping to be able to make friends with/spy on, on board.

"Maybe our mum can come and get us?" says Lolly to Mr Shaw the receptionist.

"We're trying to get hold of your parents at the moment," says Mr Shaw. "Don't worry. It's bound to be a misunderstanding."

"Of course it is!" I say cheerily, getting out a spare notebook from my bag, and my pencil case of felt-tip pens, and setting Lolly up on the coffee table in the entrance area, where she starts drawing pictures of cats and giraffes. It's quite embarrassing, standing there, while teachers talk quietly over our heads about how we will get home. I don't want them to think badly about Mum and Dad. I don't want them to think badly of *us*.

It's been nearly an hour by the time I hear Mr Shaw talking to my dad on the phone. I can't understand what's being said, but the gist of the conversations is that there is a reason Dad has been held up, and he'd been expecting us to go on the bus, and because he can't, for whatever reason, get to the school to get us, and Mum is at work, he's going to send a taxi.

Mrs Locke appears with the head teacher, Miss Manning, and they stand talking to Lolly about her drawing, and asking us questions that I know are to see if we have a happy home life, and, really, it just seems quite nosy and unnecessary.

"How is the new house?" says Miss Manning.

"Really nice," I say.

"And how are your parents settling in?"

"Really well," I say.

"What are the main differences between where you were before, and here?"

"People ask more questions," is what I want to say. But instead I say, "It's just so nice, you know. To live on a lovely new street, and make lovely new friends, and see Mum and Dad so happy to actually own their own home like they've always wanted."

They look at each other. Adults are always looking at each other, thinking kids don't know they're sending secret messages to each other.

But we do. *I* do.

"What about you?"

"I've never felt so happy," I say, and stare at them both, with the biggest smile I can possibly manage, which after a bit makes my cheeks ache. "And me and my mum are going to enter the Great Big Family Baking Competition. I'm so excited! I love baking!"

This seems to do it because they don't ask any more questions, and as much as I like Mrs Locke, I don't much feel like answering any more, either. I mean, I'm all for being nosy. Unless it's people being nosy about *me*.

When the taxi arrives, Lolly and I both get in the back, and she's telling me about this boy Jax and a girl called Abba, and how the three of them put playdough inside their shoes during story time.

"And Miss Zhao didn't notice, and we were giggling, and then she moved me and Jax apart, but me and Abba were still next to each other, and when we took the playdough out it was all warm and had the pattern of our socks on."

She starts laughing again, at the memory, and while I nod and laugh in all the right places, in truth, my head and heart are full of the baking competition. It's got to be a sign; it really has. The best thing about it is that I get to enter with Mum. She's honestly the best cook, and not just because she's my mum. Everybody who tries her cooking says so. She once made a cake that looked like a basket of flowers, with a handle and everything. The flowers looked so real my dad went to smell them when he came in from work. It was a chocolate and vanilla cake. He got chocolate icing on his nose. It tasted amazing.

I pull out my notebook and start writing down my favourite flavours.

Vanilla – obviously

Violet

Lavender

Rose

Lemon/lime

Something to do with fresh raspberries.

We could make our own lemon curd for inside the layers, if we do a layer cake. We could make it bright and glossy, thick between the layers in different colours. We could do lemon, orange and lime. We could make a...

"Why didn't anyone come and get us?" says

Lolly suddenly, not laughing any more, as I accidentally catch the taxi driver's eye in the wing mirror. She looks very tired, so I say, "It was just a mistake. Easily done, hey? Dad thought we were getting the bus." And then I suggest a game of ice-cream vans, so we pretend the back of the taxi is an ice-cream van with loads of flavours, and we can help ourselves to whatever we want, and I make Lolly a rainbow-coloured, seven-berry toffee sauce double sprinkle cone and she pretends to eat it, until we pull up outside number 16 Ridgeway Close.

When we get in, Dad is at the door, looking very sorry, and really very smart. He's wearing something different too, instead of that grey T-shirt he's been wearing for days. He's brushed his hair, and he's holding Giraffey out for Lolly, who goes bounding over to him, and lets him pick her up and swirl her about, and all I can hear is a bunch of words coming from her mouth on fast-forward, including, *snack*, *Jax*, *Abba*, *toes*, *toilet*, *dog poo*.

Dad says, "Let's go into the kitchen. I've made something nice for tea," and then he pays the taxi driver and says, "Thanks very much, mate," and the taxi driver nods and says, "Quite a couple of kids you've got yourself there."

And Dad smiles a big smile and says, "Thank you. You're right. I have." Then we all go inside.

Dad has taken the plastic covering from the sofa, and set up the living room, and it looks really amazing.

"Ta-da!" he says proudly.

I feel my heart rise, because it *does* look lovely, and he's even set it up a bit to look like the living room in our mobile home, and there's something about that which makes my tummy contract with the memory.

"Wow, Dad," I say.

Lolly goes and does a headstand on the sofa with her school shoes on and Dad doesn't tell her not to.

Dad has made us sausages and mash, with gravy and peas, and has bought new ketchup, so Lolly and I sit at the table in the dining room and start to eat, while he asks us about our day, and talks about the fact that there's a different shift pattern available at work, which would mean he would work different hours when he goes back. It would mean him being there before school, and often when we got home in the afternoon, and Lolly and I look at each other, and keep adding ketchup to our plates, and Dad doesn't say anything about too much ketchup being not very good for you, and he's just talking and talking and talking and we're chewing and nodding and trying to listen properly, but lots of his sentences are too full and he's not really making much sense for some reason.

I look at the clock. It's already five o'clock and I want to leave the house to meet Rudo.

While Dad is in such a good mood, I decide to come right out and ask him.

"Can I go outside and play with some of the kids who live on the street please, Dad? I won't go far. Just in the car park bit? Just for a while?"

Dad looks up and smiles. "I don't see why not," he says. "I was hoping you'd make some friends today. You'll need a bath too later, so how about an hour? Make sure you've got your phone on you, and don't go anywhere without telling me."

"What about me?" says Lolly. She pulls The Face. The one where her eyes go big and her bottom lip goes out, which means I usually give her whatever she wants, but this time I'm firm. I don't want to take her to the clubhouse. Not yet.

"Just by myself this time, Lollington," I say. "But we can go exploring at the weekend if Dad says yes."

"Of course," says Dad, smiling at us both. "Anyway, Lolly, I thought you wanted to play Mario Kart. I've set up the Switch."

"Yesss!" says Lolly, jumping up and rushing off into the living room.

"Thanks, Dad," I say.

"No worries at all," says Dad, and then he pauses before saying, "Do you think we made the right decision? Moving here?"

I hear a crack in his voice, just a small one that other people might not notice, and he's looking at me like I'm the adult and he's the child, so I think to myself, *What would an adult do in this situation?* Not me as an adult in this situation because I've already promised the universe that when I'm an adult I'm going to be honest with my kids and make sure they always know what's going on and not fob them off with a pretend version of things that adults think are best for children but just make everything even more confusing.

"Of course you have, Dad," I say, smiling. "It's the best decision you've ever made. You'll see." I sound so convincing even I believe it, and I see the effect it has on him, because he's beaming at me, and I think maybe that's why adults make stuff up and say stuff that's not true, to make kids smile like that and not worry. A bit like what I do with Lolly actually. But, I'd still rather have the truth, because at least the truth doesn't change and nobody can trick you with it.

"OK?" I say.

"OK," says Dad, smiling. He picks up his glass of water and takes it through to the living room. It's the first time in a long time I've seen him drink something other than coffee or beer.

I run upstairs to get my phone before I go. When I look at it there are no new messages. And the message I sent to Mum last night still hasn't been delivered. I get another feeling in my stomach. It's like I've swallowed handfuls of hot stones.

Just keep thinking of the Great Big Family Baking Competition. Just keep thinking of that.

As Lolly and Dad start shouting at each other excitedly during Mario Kart, I leave the house to meet Rudo. I look at the undelivered message to Mum on my phone again, look about the living room, and go into the kitchen and look in there too. Mum's not unpacked anything at all. It's all been Dad.

Then it hits me.

There's no sign of her, no smell of her, no *actual her*, anywhere in number 16 at all. The boxes with her personal stuff are still underneath the stairs, unopened, with her handwriting in marker pen on top of them. *Dana's things*, it says. Big and thick and navy blue.

I take the deepest breath I can possibly manage because right now I'm finding it hard to breathe let alone pretend about everything. The reason I was nervous when my teachers were asking me questions, and when Rudo wanted to come over, the truth is, I haven't seen or heard from my mum in real life for exactly five days.

CHAPTER
7

I'm still holding my breath as I step out of the front door on to Ridgeway Close and really try to work out exactly where my mum has gone. I knew she'd be busy when we moved in. I knew her new job would be long hours at first, just while she was trying to make a good impression. I knew things would be different. But. I'd expected her to be here *sometimes*. I miss her. Mum has never really been one for giving big cuddles, but she's always given good words. It's the lack of them I'm really missing.

So *where is she*? She can't be sleeping at work. She can't have just *disappeared*. But deep down I know she's not been back to the house in days. I can feel it – what *isn't* there. There's no light veil of orange oil resting in the air, there's no mug with lipstick marks round the rim sitting on the side of the kitchen waiting to be rinsed, there's no shampoo bar on the side of the bath, wrapped round with strands of her long hair after she's washed it that she's not pulled out yet. There's no smell of the curling tong, heating up, singeing the air first thing in the morning, or before she leaves the house at night.

It's like she really has disappeared. Dad would

have told us if something had happened to her, though, wouldn't he?

When I get to the back of the fence that leads to the show home garden I wonder if Rudo's there already, or if I should wait for him here. I decide to wait, just for a bit, pretending I'm not really waiting for anybody. Thoughts of Mum are whizzing about in my head, like I know more than my brain is letting on, but it just won't tell me for some reason.

So instead I focus on the woman from number 12, who's heaving her green wheelie bin out on to the corner. It looks really full and heavy and I wonder what's in there. It's so heavy she can hardly get it to move along, and I see her muttering to herself. If this was a detective story, there would be evidence inside her bin. I'll ask Rudo if he thinks we should take a look inside. I still can't see any sign of children living there. Perhaps she locks her children in the cellar. *Thanks, brain, let's not go there.* But even thinking about that is better than thinking about where my mum is.

It's very easy to make assumptions about what the woman from number 12 might have inside her bin after seeing her sawing in her bedroom last night. *Maybe it's a dead body*, I think, and then shake my head. It's probably some offcuts of wood from some DIY she was doing. What was it Miss Younger used to say to me at my old school? "Now come on, Luna, let's not catastrophise…" I had to look that word up. It meant turning a simple worry or event into something really big and over the top. It makes me cross to think of that. If anything I do the opposite. I *de*-catastrophise. I *un*-catastrophise. I'm *anti-catastrophic*. I didn't bother telling Miss Younger that, though. Some adults only see what they want to see and have no idea what children are thinking about at all.

I look at my phone. It's 17.32. Rudo is probably already there. I hate being late for anything, even hastily made plans with no definite timescale, so I pull over the same tub that Rudo used and leap up on to it, heave my leg over the badly made fence, and slither down into the garden on the other side.

Immediately I realise something is different, so I duck down behind a big planter full of plastic flowers that's taller than Lolly. Over by the patio doors Greg Martin has stepped out into the garden with a couple, and they are talking about what it's like to live on Ridgeway Close.

"It's just wonderful to see families thriving here," Greg Martin says, in that special voice of his that he saves for potential customers. "Already we've got lots of children hopping about the place. My own children would love to live here. They keep trying to convince me. The only thing that's putting me off is how I'd feel about living so near to work… Still, it never feels like work in a place like this! So you never know … we could be neighbours one day!"

My heart is beating fast. What if they find me here? What if I get Mum and Dad into trouble? What if Greg Martin really is a villain, and he captures me and locks me up somewhere and nobody knows where I am until it's too late? What if he gives me to the woman at number 12…? *Now come on, Luna*, I say to myself in Miss Younger's voice, *let's not catastrophise…*

I take deep breaths, like that doctor I used to have to go to once showed me, and I huddle up in a ball, making myself as small as I possibly can. Today is one of those days that I'd like to pack up and kick to the moon. I wonder if Rudo's in the clubhouse and can see me hiding. I wonder if he thinks I'm a scaredy-cat, and the thought that he might makes me feel one hundred times worse.

"We weren't sure if we wanted a new build," says the woman with Greg Martin. "I've always liked houses with a bit of history."

"Ah, well! Lots of people say that when they come here. They're weighing up whether to go new, or to find something with character. That's what they call it. But can I show you all these lovely Edwardian details our architects have incorporated into the structure of these new builds?"

Greg Martin sounds so disgustingly cheery that I am almost tempted to stand up and shout, "Don't believe this man. He's just trying to get your money. Run! Run to the hills!" but I don't, of course.

"I do love the little brass outdoor light fittings," says the woman.

"Yes, and have you noticed the shape of the windows?" says the man.

"Yes!" says the woman. "It's obviously not a period house, but it's definitely got *something*.

How much would it cost to have the garden fitted out like this one? With the same things?"

"Well," says Greg Martin in a way that makes me imagine his big swirling eyes as he draws them to him, "let's go inside and take a look. We do have a sales option that includes all furniture, a choice of decor and an entirely cultivated and landscaped garden…"

"Imagine that," says the man. "Moving in and not having to do a thing."

"Imagine!" says the woman, and then the three of them are back inside the house and I hear the back door shut behind them.

I let out the breath it feels like I've been holding for seventy years and feel my body crumple up like a balloon that's been let go halfway through being blown up, all flat and whizzed out and soggy.

Gosh, I hate Greg Martin. Were these the things he said to my mum and dad, standing in the house with the flagpoles out front and the glossy plastic vegetables? Which one of them had heard his words and thought, yes, this is *exactly* what we need. Which one of them was to blame for this 100% shambles? If Mum actually *was* here, I might even shout at her.

Once my breath has calmed down and my heart isn't beating so fast that it feels it's going to burst out of my chest and bounce away along the garden, I start to crawl to the back entrance of the tree house. It's actually very easy to move through this garden without being seen, but the thought of being caught still terrifies me.

I shimmy up the ladder, pull myself up and open the door, excited to see Rudo and hoping that he saw how well I dealt with nearly being caught by Greg Martin, but the clubhouse is empty. There's no Rudo making hot chocolate or lounging about on the sofa. The kettle is empty. I look in the little bin and there are the two torn packets that had held the hot chocolate.

I try not to be too disappointed. Rudo hadn't promised he'd come. He'd said he'd try. I know more than most people that things can come up unexpectedly that stop you from doing what you want to do. I know sometimes kids have no say in these things. And I can't actually remember if we ever agreed an exact time to meet. Maybe Rudo thought we'd sneak outside later at night.

I look in my backpack. I've packed jelly snakes

and a cheese sandwich. I get them out and put them on the coffee table. There's a cardboard carton of apple juice in the backpack, so I get that out too and stab the metal circle with the straw. I'll take my rubbish home, including the hot chocolate sachets from yesterday. I know nobody comes up here – how would an adult even climb up the ladder into the tree? – but we still need to be really careful.

Then I get out my notebook and my colouring pencils and my best blue biro, which is super smooth and makes my writing look actually really neat for a change. I refuse to do joined-up writing at home even though we have to do it at school in order to pass our SATs. Nobody said we had to have one kind of handwriting all the time, did they?

I open a new page and write the title.

THE GREAT BIG FAMILY BAKING COMPETITION. LUNA AND DANA LOVERIDGE.

In the middle of the page I write UNDER THE SEA and draw a wave shape round it. Then I draw an arrow coming out of the wave and then another and another. At the tip of each arrow I write a different idea. My aim is to have a whole page of ideas to show Mum when I see her later, so together we can think of how we'll go about winning the competition.

I draw and write and draw and write. Word after word and picture after picture fill up lots of pages. My brain is full of waves and mermaids and pirates and seaweed and golden doubloons. I imagine a seahorse with a long shimmery tail. You can get that spray-on colour for cakes that makes it look like that. Or maybe I should just do fish, lots of different-flavoured cakes. Orange, lemon, lime, with homemade curd in the centre, each little cake made to look like a different type of tropical fish. I open up the browser on my phone and type in the words *small tropical fish* and choose *images*. The screen fills up with bright creatures that would make perfect little cakes.

Livebearer, guppy, Siamese lightning fish, tetra, neon tetra, killifish, cherry barb, zebra fish, catfish, green swordtail, platy.

Imagine a fish tank made of boiled-down clear Glacier Mint sweets, spread smooth and cooled to look like sheets of glass. Imagine the tank full of little tropical fish, all bright and decorated beautifully. Each one a different flavour. Imagine coloured stones on the floor of the tank, all made of flavoured marzipan like the fruit on a simnel cake. Imagine one of those little castles you get in home aquariums, but this one's a cake made of sponge bricks and stuck together with flavoured butter icing...

"Mum!" I call out to myself. "I think I've got it!"

I can see the cakes in my mind. I start to imagine the flavours too. Cinnamon. Ginger. Cardamom. Lime.

When I look at the page of my book it's covered in drawings and words and excited writing. My phone says it's seven o'clock. I'd better get home. Mum and Dad will worry.

I hope Rudo is all right.

CHAPTER 8

At school we practise for our SATs every morning, and I stare at the reasoning question like it's written upside down. It's when they put questions into little stories I find them hard. I get into the story, and then at the end I realise I'm supposed to be working something out from the information I've been given. But my brain doesn't work like that.

I look up at the whiteboard. Mrs Locke has written down some top tips when approaching a SATs maths question.

1. Read it slowly and several times.
2. Work out what it's asking you.
3. What do you know?
4. What do you need to know?
5. What can you do to find out?
ALSO:
6. Show each stage of your working out.
7. Show your answer clearly in the right box.
   How hard could it be?

Too hard. I'm more interested in what happens to the characters Romesh and Carly, who've been given fifty-six sweets between them in the first place, rather than whatever it is I'm being asked about percentages.

"You can do this, Luna," says Mrs Locke over

my shoulder. "What are the key words in the question?"

I read the question carefully again.

"Imagine the words you need in order to work out the sum popping out at you, like they're on a spring. That's what I do," she says, and smiles kindly. So kindly I nearly want to tell her about my mum, but luckily I think better of it.

Rudo isn't here. I'm worried about him. First he didn't show up at the clubhouse last night, then he wasn't on the bus this morning, and now he's not here either. Mrs Locke didn't even call his name out on the register.

"Where's your boyfriend?" says Jennifer Browne smugly. But I know her game. I've played it a zillion times at my old school. She wants me to say, "He's not my boyfriend!" and get upset so she can wind me up about it, but I don't get upset or angry or cross with her. I just say, "He's not here yet," and I see the look on her face, which says, *Luna Loveridge has just admitted Rudo is her boyfriend and isn't that bothered about me knowing about it, so what do I say to wind her up now then?* And I smile sweetly and look back at the next maths question.

Hannah's watch shows five minutes past nine.
Hannah's watch is twelve minutes slow.
What is the real time?

Well, I need to do five minutes past nine subtract twelve minutes. So … that's minus seven. No. Wait. Is this a trick question? That seems too easy. Hours are sixty minutes, not one hundred. Does that have anything to do with it? It's DEFINITELY a subtraction question … isn't it? URGH, brain. If I was baking a basic Victoria sponge cake, how long would each seven-inch tin take, and would there be a difference at the top or the bottom of the new oven? I haven't had a chance to try it out yet. If all the maths questions were about baking cakes, I'd be a whizz at them.

"Did you do maths SATs practice at your old school?" says Mrs Locke gently behind me, looking at the doodles on my paper of an oven and a cake tin and a big question mark I've outlined in swirly biro.

"Yes," I say. "But I didn't really understand it then either."

"It's OK," says Mrs Locke kindly. "I reckon we'll get you finding your own pace in no time. Would you like to go with the group who sits in the den area with Mr Waits?"

I am not sure if I do. Mr Waits is the teaching assistant and I've not had a conversation with him yet.

"Maybe..." I say, so I'm not committing to anything.

"I'll get him to come and speak to you," she says. "He can tell you what they do out there, and you can decide if it will help you or not."

"That's really nice," I say, surprised. "At my old school they just told you what to do." Mrs Locke laughs. "Oh, we do that too ... but not in this instance."

Jennifer Browne isn't going to give up on me just yet. When Mrs Locke has moved on she leans over and says, "Your boyfriend is rubbish at maths too."

I don't say anything.

"Maybe you can have extra lessons together. For people who are rubbish at stuff."

I still don't say anything. I think of the sweets in the first question and imagine them wrapped in brightly coloured paper. I wonder what flavour they are.

"She's concentrating," says the boy next to her.

His name is Jared Stocks. "You can tell because she's dribbling."

The two of them laugh. I think, very carefully, about what the best thing is to say in this situation. Adults at my old school gave me lots of advice about what to do when people were being mean to me, how to behave differently, what to say. None of it worked, and it always got me in a muddle. I thought of Mum, and what she said.

"You could ignore it if you think you can. You could try to please them, but I promise you that won't make you feel any better. You could tell an adult you trust."

I put my hand up. Mrs Locke comes over and Jennifer and Jared get on with their work.

"Can I talk to you?" I say as quietly as I can. "In private."

"Of course."

At the front of the classroom I think of all the things I could tell Mrs Locke. I could say, *I don't think my dad's coping very well at the minute and that's why he keeps forgetting things.* I could say, *I'm really worried about Rudo; do you know if he's OK? I saw him sneaking about the night before last in the dark.* Or I could say, *I haven't seen my mum for nearly a week – and, yes, she's disappeared before for a night or two, one time for three nights, I think, but I didn't notice until the second night – but she's never gone away for this long before and I'm worried I've done something really awful to make her leave me and that it's all my fault. Can you tell me how to be better at being a human being so she comes back?* This thought is too much, so I try to think of decorated sponge-cake fish bobbing about in a prize-winning cake aquarium. And instead, I say, "Ever since I got here Jennifer has been horrible to me, and she was just making fun of me being bad at maths, and is there any way I can move somewhere else please?"

Mrs Locke smiles at me sympathetically. "Of course," she says.

"Can you not make it obvious that I said something?" I say. "It's just…"

"I know," says Mrs Locke. "But, you know, we don't accept that sort of thing here. The problem won't be fixed by moving you. The head teacher is very firm about it. So I will be having a word with her, and making sure it doesn't happen again. But also, you have to tell me if it does. Is that OK?"

I suppose her response means that Mrs Locke is trying to prove she's *an adult I can trust*.

When I'm back in my seat I read through the question slowly, very slowly, and try to work out what I already know, even if it's only a tiny thing. At least it's a step towards an answer.

I try to show my workings at the same time I imagine the sort of piping I could do on a cherry barb fish. Me and Mum have got a huge box of nozzles and icing bags. The first time she ever taught me to ice it was on row after row of rich tea biscuits. It didn't matter if I made a mess of them. I was learning. When I'd finished, and I looked at them on the old kitchen counter, I felt like I could achieve anything. The smile she gave me was like winning every competition in the world.

When a bit of time has passed Mrs Locke comes over and moves me to another table. She makes it look like it was her idea, randomly, because she moves some other children slightly around too, and I want to jump up and down saying *thank you thank you thank you*. But instead I nod at her and look over at Jennifer Browne who is whispering to Jared and looking over at me. I can't wait until Rudo comes back. At least I know they definitely *won't* be joining our club.

As I settle into my new seat, Mr Shaw, the receptionist, appears at the classroom door with a folder and talks quietly with Mrs Locke. She is nodding seriously, and I wish I could hear what they were talking about.

"I'm Meg," says the girl in the space next to me.

"I'm Luna," I say.

"Do you like skipping?"

"With a rope?"

"Yeah!"

"I guess so. Yes." It's been a long time since I tried, but I don't say that.

"Want to play with me and Tish at break?" She nods to the girl in the opposite seat who's holding ice-cream cone highlighters and colouring little dots. "And Brynn." She nods at the boy next to Tish, who is leaning over his work and drawing lots of intricate workings out in pencil. He looks up and nods at me and then looks down.

"Maths is Brynn's favourite," says Meg in explanation.

"Yes please," I say. I'm tempted to say no thank you, and stand by myself in the corner of the playground where I know I'll be safe, but I know that's not really what I want, not deep down. What I want is to make some friends and not worry about people tricking or laughing at me. And I won't be able to do that if I don't take a few little risks like this.

"There's these really long ropes so two of you can jump at the same time. We need another person so we've got two to hold the rope and two to jump," says Meg.

"Great," I say, feeling glad that I said something to Mrs Locke. I'm about to say something else when Mr Shaw looks over at me, and Mrs Locke says, "Luna, we need to borrow you for a moment. In reception. Nothing to worry about." She smiles one of those smiles adults do when there is *lots* to worry about. Never trust an adult who says there's nothing to worry about. Rule number one.

"You'll need to take your things."

"See you at break?" says Meg, smiling, and I smile back.

"You will!" I promise.

As Mr Shaw leads me along the corridor he turns to say, "Please don't worry, it's just your dad needs to pick you up early today for various reasons. You'll be back in tomorrow as usual. Nothing to worry about."

Adults should carry signs that say "Nothing to worry about!" on them, and on the back say "Except all the things we haven't explained to you or told you about and are keeping secret". But I don't say that. I just try to stop the feeling in my chest where my heart is beating too fast. Remember to count, remember to breathe. Sometimes that is easier said than done. *Now come on, Luna, let's not catastrophise.* Thanks, Miss Younger. I'm so glad you are in my head to make me feel even worse at times like this.

Oh no! I think suddenly. Meg is expecting me to play at break and if I don't turn up, then I may have missed my chance at making a new group of friends. This thought nearly tips me over the edge and I have to bite my tongue to stop from crying.

There's a woman in reception, standing with my dad, who's next to Lolly. I've not seen her before, but she looks familiar. She's got long hair in cornrows and plaits and she's wearing a striped dress of green and yellow. She's bending down, saying something to Lolly, who is nodding and holding up Giraffey.

Dad is dressed up all smartly, in a suit and tie, which is strange, as he never ever dresses like that, except for when we went to Nanna's funeral. He's holding a bunch of flowers too, two long strips of gladioli like we used to grow in our old garden, yellow and orange, like sunbeams. He's looking proud of himself, though, so I just say, "Wow, Dad, you look smart!" even though inside I'm vibrating with worry, and he says, "Thank you very much!" and a smile breaks through, like someone's turned on a street lamp.

I can see that he's shaking.

"Hello," I say to the woman in the stripy dress. "Who are you?" This is what Miss Younger used to call my "getting to the point" voice. She said some people don't like it when I am so abrupt and I should practise easing into the conversation. I've practised that, but it goes even worse than if I talk like this. I realise one of the things I like about Rudo is he didn't seem to misunderstand the way I talk, right from the very beginning.

"Hello," she says. "I'm Odelia."

"You're not a doctor, are you?" I had more than my fill of doctors at the old house, when I had to see those ones about when I start to panic. It's not that they weren't helpful, but there isn't time for me to talk about my problems at the minute. That would just get in the way.

"No," she says kindly. "I'm Rudo's mum. Please don't worry, but he's hurt himself and is in hospital," she says. "Your dad has agreed that you can go and visit him. We've talked about what good friends you've become."

I am staring at her, not *watching*, this time. I have several thoughts. Rudo is in hospital. Our parents know we are friends, when I'm pretty sure I've not mentioned a single thing about him. Maybe my spying isn't so secret after all.

Rudo is in hospital. I knew something was wrong.

"I've got to go near the hospital too," says Dad. "I've got ... a meeting about those new shift hours. I thought it would be easier if we all went in that direction together. I can come and find you when I'm done. It's not far. It's all cleared with Miss Manning."

"Is Rudo OK?" I feel my heart scratch inside my ribcage like a small animal trying to escape. I knew something was up with Rudo. I hold on to Lolly, leaning down to lift her up so I can feel her head on my shoulder. She's trying to show Giraffey how to stick his tongue up his nose by giving him the perfect example.

"Honestly, he's fine," says Odelia, taking Lolly's hand. "Nothing to worry about."

Oh great. Nothing to worry about. What if Rudo is in lots of pain? What if he's not going to make it through the night? *What if he's already dead?*

"Are you all right, Luna?" Dad pulls me to him, and I'm crushed against the cellophane surrounding the gladioli. "Just take a deep breath."

I do as I'm told. *Now come on, Luna, let's not catastrophise.*

I feel sick but my heart starts to slow down. Then I realise what Dad said to me.

"That's great, Dad!" This explains the suit. But not the flowers. "What hours are they again?"

"Earlies," he says, quickly.

"How early?"

"Not sure exactly," says Dad, and I raise an eyebrow at him. "Early enough that I'd be done when you two finish school," he adds. "I just need to make sure they know I'm serious about it." He sets his jaw to the side like he does when he's really concentrating on something.

"Well, the suit should do it," I say encouragingly. He does look impressive. I haven't seen him make this much effort in ages.

We get into Rudo's mum's car and it smells like him a bit. There are a pair of tap shoes on the back seat, too. They've got black ribbons as laces and metal plates on the toes and heels, and Rudo's name written inside them in red biro. There's a notebook next to them and I pick it up and look inside. There are drawings all over the pages, like the drawings on the visual timetable in our classroom, and that's when I realise just how good Rudo is. He really played his artistic side down.

I drop it quickly because he hasn't given me permission to look at it, and I'm really funny about people looking at my notebooks too. In the front his mum must have noticed, because she says, "Oh, don't worry about looking at that."

"I'd rather have permission," I say, truthfully.

"Well, that's very commendable," laughs Rudo's mum. "But when we get there, make sure

to ask him why he's in hospital in the first place."
She shakes her head. "I'm surprised your dad is
still happy for you to be friends."

Dad turns and smiles at me. "We know a few
people who've made some interesting decisions
in life, don't we, kids?"

I nod. He's right. We do.

Lolly is bouncing Giraffey in her lap and talking
quietly to herself in her car seat beside me. I
open Rudo's notebook again. There are all sorts
of drawings, some of fish and whales and others
that are just really big colourful lettering, saying
things like STOP and NO MORE and HUMANS
SHOULD THINK. Then I get to a page where
there are dates and times, a bit like my notebook
and I realise these are Rudo's own spying-on-the-
people-of-Ridgeway-Close notes.

Monday a.m.: spot new girl from number 16 on
the kerb. She's writing in a notebook and staring at
Greg Martin who is being slimy. Think she's taking
notes.

This makes me laugh. That was the day we met.
I want to add a note to Rudo's, saying, *I wasn't
staring; I was watching*, but I don't.

Monday a.m.: introduced myself to the new girl.

She's called Luna and I decided to show her the clubhouse. I like her.

This makes my cheeks feel hot. I think I shouldn't be reading this, but I turn the page over once more, just to see if there's anything else about me.

Monday p.m.: Paula at number 12 is obviously some kind of murderer because she's STILL sawing stuff. WHAT IS SHE DOING? I'm going to investigate further. Keep an eye on M.

Ha! Exactly what I thought. Although I still haven't spotted her daughter. Maybe she keeps her in the cellar...?

Very early hours of Tuesday morning: the new woman at number 16, Luna's mum, is standing outside the front of the house looking up at the windows. She's holding something I can't see because it's dark, and it looks like she's crying. Really crying. She looks like the saddest person in the world.

I slam the book closed quickly. I don't want to read any more. I shouldn't have read it to begin with. There's a mistake, somehow. I'd have noticed if Mum had been standing in front of the house crying in the early hours of the morning. I notice *everything*.

"Right!" says Rudo's mum cheerily. "We're here."

She pulls the car into the hospital car park and we drive about for a while trying to find a space. Dad is smoothing his hair in the pull-down mirror, looking nervous. Lolly is in her own world with Giraffey.

Rudo was mistaken. He never saw my mum. Maybe it was a postwoman. Maybe it was someone on their way somewhere. Maybe...

In my head I imagine mine and Mum's entry into the Great Big Family Baking Competition. Me and Mum standing behind a big glass tank made of melted Glacier Mints, full of hanging cake fish and a cake castle rising up from the bottom, and seaweed made of spun sugar. Little zebra fish and cherry barbs and lightning fish. Ginger. Cardamom. Lime. I can see it so clearly. Me and Mum winning a big shiny trophy, being handed our prize in a big envelope, and Jennifer Browne and her mum standing in front of a slumped cake that the judges described as "a foul, inedible mess", which makes Jennifer cry, while her mum, who in my imagination is just her but taller and in a suit, gives her a heated-up sausage roll to try to make her feel better.

I slip my phone out of my pocket. ♥ you, Mum. Can you make sure you wake me up when you get home from work please? I haven't seen you in days. I miss you x

I send the text and it doesn't show as delivered, just like the others. I've got to stay strong and plan our entry to the competition. There has to be a good reason that I've not seen her. She'd never just go off and leave us. Not again. Not for this long.

Would she?

CHAPTER
9

Rudo's hospital bed is in a long ward with other kids, but there's a curtain that goes all the way round it to give him his privacy. I'm glad his mum has taken Lolly to the park and given us time alone, and Dad has gone to work to talk about his new hours, because I really want to know what's happened to him. I have the feeling it won't be the full version if anyone else is there. I gasp when I see him. He's all bandaged up, in a sort of hoist thing that's wrapped round his middle, with one leg in plaster hanging in the air, like you see when people have hurt themselves on TV. He looks really poorly, even though he's smiling at me.

"What on earth happened to you?" I say angrily. I don't mean to sound angry; it's just he really matters to me and I don't want him to not be here any more. He's the best thing that's happened in so long, and I could cry seeing him there, all wrapped up and kept still like that. He's got his hair down and long over his shoulders and is wearing a different-coloured headband to usual. He smiles softly and shrugs.

"Hello to you. It's a long story," he says.

"I'm here for an hour, so there's time," I say,

tapping my fingers on the corner of the metal frame, pretending to be impatient. I smile at him, though. It's such a relief to see him. "Start with what's actually wrong with you. From where I'm standing you look like you've broken yourself all over."

"Well…" he says. "I *do* have a broken collarbone, something broken in my leg, and a light puncture wound to my ribcage that needed late surgery to fix up a bit."

I put my hand to my mouth.

"It's all OK," he reassures me quickly, even though it should be me doing the reassuring. "Kids' bones heal much faster than adults. I'll probably be tap-dancing again by next week."

I tut. But I'm glad he's still Rudo. "But how did it happen?"

"You know I said I like sneaking…" He pulls a sheepish look.

"Yes…"

"I had this idea," he says, grinning now. "You know the bridge the school bus goes under? The one people hang rubbish homemade banners on that say things like HAPPY 50th, SUE! and WELL

DONE FOR PASSING YOUR DRIVING TEST, DUNCAN?"

I can't think of the bridge, but I know the kinds of banners he means. They used to hang them on the wall outside the pub in our old village, and people would add rude words to them if they were up there too long.

"Sort of," I say.

"And you know I said I like … murals? Well. For the past few months I've been going out early, or sometimes late, to spray-paint my own banner straight on to the concrete."

I stare at him. He looks so pleased with himself, despite sitting in a hospital bed.

"You … what?" So it *was* him sneaking out of his house late at night. To perform acts of vandalism!

"I wanted to get people in this town thinking," he says very seriously. "People don't think much. I thought I'd … give them a push."

"Where did you get the idea from?

"YouTube."

"Rudo!"

"You haven't even asked me what it said yet," he says. He pulls himself up a bit higher in the bed and winces.

"What did it say?" I'm still trying to imagine how he got up there. Did he dangle off or over the bridge? Did he climb on to something? Did he fall and that's how he hurt himself? What on earth possessed him to do something so dangerous?

"It said SAVE THE WHALES," says Rudo, smiling.

"Save them from what?"

"Extinction. Plastic pollution. Human beings in general."

"Well, that's admirable, but isn't…"

"I was using environmentally friendly paint, before you ask."

I smile at him. "You think of everything. Weren't you scared?" It's impossible to be angry with Rudo.

"When I fell?" he says.

"No. Going out late at night on your own. Anything could have happened and nobody would have known where you were."

"I wasn't scared," he says quietly, then he points to a bucket of popcorn on the table and says, "Have some of that, and pass me some, will you, please?"

"What about when you fell?" I say, as we both

tuck into the popcorn. It's the toffee kind, the stuff I like. I suddenly realise I'm really hungry.

"I was scared then," says Rudo. "I guess I've been doing a few things without thinking them through recently."

"Why?"

"I want to prove to Mum I'm more grown-up than she thinks I am. She's so protective of me. Ever since Dad died..." Rudo trails off. "She worries. A lot. I wanted to prove to her she didn't need to. I got my save the planet stuff from her. She's taken me to so many protests and things over the years. I just wanted her to stop seeing me as a baby who needs protecting at all costs."

"Well, you did a good job of proving that, Rudo," I say, as kindly as I can. "And I'm sorry about your dad."

"Oh, it's OK," says Rudo. "I mean, it's not OK. I do miss him. I miss Mum being relaxed sometimes. I really worried her this time." He shakes his head. "I'm going to have to think of some other ways to change the world that don't involve me ending up in hospital and my mum being really upset, aren't I?"

"I think so."

I think about Rudo's mum in her stripy dress, tall and kind-looking, the way she was gentle with Lolly so that I didn't have to calm her myself. I tried to imagine what Rudo's dad might have been like.

"You can talk to me whenever you like," I say. "About your dad."

"Thanks," says Rudo. "I mostly don't want to. But sometimes I might." He smiles. I smile. We both eat more popcorn.

I suddenly want to ask him about what I saw in his notebook. About Mum, standing outside our house at night-time crying. I want to tell him I haven't seen her for nearly two weeks now, and I have absolutely no idea what's happened to her – if she's run away, or had an accident, or just had enough of being my mum because I'm just so terrible at being her daughter. *Was she OK when you saw her? Did you see where she went?* But I don't say that. I don't say anything, and just eat more popcorn.

I think of the letters I write to my little sister from my mum, so Lolly doesn't know that she's sort of disappeared and doesn't have to feel all the worry I feel. How I make myself breakfast and pretend my mum made it before she's gone to work, not just for Lolly. I make pancakes with smiley faces and say, "Thank you, Mum!" even though I've made them myself. I take a deep breath. I can't think about these things at the moment.

"I'm glad you're all right," I say cheerfully. "I know we've only just met, but I don't want some news programme to inform me that LOCAL BOY DIES HANGING OFF BRIDGE, thank you very much. So when you're better, make sure you're more careful next time." I don't bother telling him not to have a next time, because I think I know Rudo well enough by now, even in the short time since I've met him, to know there's no point telling him what he should and shouldn't do.

"I didn't even fall off the bridge," he says, still smiling. "I sort of tripped over my backpack on the way home, climbing over a fence to do a shortcut, and landed on a metal fence spike."

I roll my eyes. I can't help it.

"I know. I know. Lesson learned. I won't go sneaking about at night. OK? I couldn't do that to Mum again anyway. I've never seen her that upset before. Not even when Dad died. That's the bit I feel bad about. So no more late-night sneaking for me."

"Good," I say. "Did the police speak to you?"

Rudo nods.

"What did they say?"

"That I shouldn't do it again, and it's illegal. They said I'd get my mum into trouble." He shakes his head and points over to the cupboard next to the bed. "Let's open some chocolates," he says, as I open the cupboard and bring out a big box of Roses. "I don't want her to get in trouble. So I promised I wouldn't do it again. And I won't. Not in *that* way, anyway." He actually winks at me, and I wonder if he'll ever do what he's told. I kind of hope he doesn't. I like him just the way he is. Even if it means he's had to be bandaged up and stay in hospital.

"What are we going to do about the clubhouse?" I say, a little sadly. "We've only just started. Who am I going to be nosy about and collect information on all the dodgy residents of Ridgeway Close with now?"

Rudo smiles. "Well," he said, "I thought maybe you could come and visit me as much as possible, and bring notes."

"Notes?"

"Yeah. Like written notes, showing who's up to what and what evidence you find and all the nosy stuff like that."

"I'd enjoy doing that," I say. I really would. "And it would mean you can help me get ready for the Great Big Family Baking Competition... I can go over my ideas with you. If you'll let me."

"Of course! It's a win-win!"

"You seem awfully cheery for someone who's been caught doing illegal activities after falling on to a railing and skewering yourself," I say, taking one of the chocolates.

"Got to see the bright side of things," says Rudo. "And the only bit I regret about it is upsetting my mum. The rest I'd do again in a heartbeat."

We both laugh. I have to admire his guts. I mean, I have to. I'm so relieved that he's OK, and that he wants to spend time with me, and that the clubhouse isn't over.

"Right, so I'll make notes, and bring them to you, and you can help me work out what's what?"

"Yup. What do you think?"

"I wanted to ask you about a few kids at school actually," I say.

"Not Jennifer and Jared? Because they are

definitely NOT joining the club," says Rudo.

"No, no, not them. I got Mrs Locke to move me today. I'm at a table with Meg, Tish and Brynn now."

"Ah, they're all right," says Rudo, shrugging. "And you're in luck. Meg lives down our street."

I stare at him, open-mouthed. I think of all the house numbers, and all the different people, and can't for a minute work out where she might live on Ridgeway Close. And I call myself a Great Baker Detective. For the sake of the competition I hope my baking's better than my detecting.

Dad appears then, with Rudo's mum and Lolly. He looks like he's been crying and for a moment I worry that something terrible has happened and he's going to be sad all evening.

"I didn't get the new hours," he says, quickly and almost too cheerfully and unexpectedly, and I know there's something off, but I have no idea what it is.

"Oh, I'm sorry, Dad," I say. "We don't mind catching the bus home!"

"It's fine," says Dad. "I'll keep asking. It's made me realise I really want something different. Maybe a different job at some point. A new challenge that fits round you two." I think of the crunched-up beer cans and how Dad is so down in the morning. I think of the arguments between him and Mum. I think of our life and what we moved away from and what we've moved to and I can see how unhappy Mum and Dad both really are, no matter how many pancakes I make.

"The good news is Odelia has agreed to have you girls after school, and bring you to the hospital so you can see Rudo each day. If you'd like to. And because I've still got a couple of weeks off work, I can take Lolly to the park."

"I'd like that," says Rudo.

"I'd like that too," I say, and all the worry of the past hour seems to fade away. As we turn to leave I say, "Which house does Meg live at then?"

Rudo wiggles his eyebrows up and down mischievously. "Number twelve."

The posh house on the corner. The one with the woman sawing.

I feel my stomach drop. For someone who prides themselves on watching people, I seem to miss out on so much information.

CHAPTER
10

Sometimes in life you have to just take the bull by the horns. That's something Mum says, or used to say, in the old house, and I take it to mean that sometimes you have to take action instead of waiting for someone else to give you permission to make it happen for you.

So that's what I have decided to do.

I've been up since five o'clock practising making little stripy zebra fish with ingredients we already had in the house. The first batch came out crumbly, black and white chunks that I put into a little paper bag to take to Rudo later. I finally find a way to do it. To cook a striped batter in a tray, like a tray bake, then cut the fish shapes out of it. I can stick any extra pieces on to the main shape with butter cream when I do it for real.

With only a few days till the Great Big Family Baking Competition, I'm going to have to get everything ready myself, and fill Mum in as soon as I find out where she is. Later today I'm going to ask Dad outright, "Where is Mum? Tell me please." And he'll tell me because I never ask for anything and the shock of me asking will get the truth out of him. I'm also going to talk to Lolly because I feel bad about making everything seem normal – or better than normal – just so she won't worry. I'd hate if people were doing that to me, and even though Lolly's little, she's still a person who deserves to be treated with respect.

I set my alarm early, long before Dad and Lolly are awake. I check in on Mum and Dad's room and Dad is snoring gently. He's still wearing part of his suit from yesterday. I make a note in my notebook to remind him to take care of himself a bit better. At least there are no empty beer cans on the bedside table. Some people shouldn't drink beer. My dad is one of them. He doesn't get really drunk and angry like you see on TV programmes. It's just … he gets sad and moody the next day, unable to smile enough to make the day nice for anyone. Unable to make breakfast with a smile on his face or make me and Lolly feel like life is a good thing to be part of and celebrate.

I sit at the kitchen table with a glass of milk and some toast with raspberry jam on. It's the final jar from last year's batch, which me and Mum made together. It's got a little label with her handwriting stuck to the side. *Summer Jam. Dana and Luna's secret recipe.* I remember her writing that on the side. We promised not to tell anyone our secret ingredient (cloves, so the jam tastes summery but with a hint of winter). I take a big bite of the toast and swallow it without really chewing it. I feel it scratching my throat on the way down and take a big gulp of milk.

The application form for the Great Big Family Baking Competition is out in front of me, and when I've licked my fingers I take the lid off a pen and fill it in.

South Downs Junior School
The Great Big Family Baking Competition
Team Application

Team name: The Macarons
Team members: Dana Loveridge (34, mum) and Luna Rae Loveridge (10, daughter, Year Six)
Your bake:

I open my notebook and look at all the drawings I did when I was alone in the clubhouse. I know me and Mum haven't talked about it, but I think she'll agree to the fish-tank idea. It will look so fantastic and taste amazing if we get it just right. I will spend as much of the next few days I can practising without her. I know I can do it. She'll be so proud of me.

Your bake: a fish tank made of melted Glacier Mints filled with a range of tropical fish, a sponge brick castle, spun-sugar seaweed and coloured marzipan stones on the tank floor. Main flavours: lemon, lime, lavender, vanilla. Ginger, cardamom and gingerbread bricks. Treasure chest with mystery-flavour golden coins.

I reread what I've written and make a note in my notebook of everything I'll need for a practice bake. I'll need to work out recipes and amounts, and a shopping list. If I ask Dad, I could do an online order, or I could go to the shop with my rucksack and get everything I need.

There's no time to waste. All Mum would have to do is turn up and enjoy herself. I send her another text.

Mum, I've entered us into a baking competition at school. The theme is 'under the sea'. I've got a BRILLIANT IDEA. You'll love it! Please tell me where you are. I know you've not been home. I'm not angry. But I need to know. X

I don't even look to see if it's been delivered. I'm going to carry on like she's reading them, and trust she's reading them, and that everything else is going to turn out all right.

I make a cup of coffee and take it up to Dad. I put it on the bedside table, and give him a few taps on the shoulder, then I come downstairs and I make a batter for pancakes and cook three thick ones, American style, and put them on a plate. And then I put raspberries and blueberries on the plate too, in a face with a big blob of yoghurt. I put some squash in a jug and put that in the middle of the table. I put two slices of bread in the toaster and go back upstairs.

"Dad..." I say, shaking him gently on the arm. "Dad."

He doesn't move at all.

"Dad!" I shout a bit now, right near his ear. I feel a flash of anger that he gets to lie here as though he hasn't got a care in the world when Lolly needs getting ready for school. And I need him. And maybe so does Mum.

"Whwrrmffhh." Dad makes a funny half-awake sound into his pillow.

"Dad, it's seven o'clock. I'm about to wake up

Lolly. There's a coffee here. I need you to get up so you can say bye-bye to Lolly and get her off to school. I've made her pancakes."

I see Dad open one eye and look straight at me. Like a whale in one of Rudo's drawings in his notebook.

"Oh, has Mum already left?"

I stare at him then. Not watching, not looking, but staring. If he's going to lie to me about where Mum is, I'm going to make him feel uncomfortable about it.

"Dad, I'm not stupid. Later on you're going to tell me where Mum is and you're not going to make stuff up."

"She's just busy at work," he says quickly, sitting up in bed. "Like I told you."

"Dad," I say firmly, "you need to tell me the truth." It feels good to say this.

"OK, Luna," says Dad. "We'll talk about this later." He shakes his head. "I'll try."

"Right." I'm not going to argue with him. I like trying to look after Dad. But sometimes, lots of times, I'd like someone to look after me, too.

"I'm going to put on a load of washing," I say, as he opens his other eye. "And I need you to hang it out, or turn the tumble dryer on or something. And then I need you to come downstairs and make Lolly feel like she's the best person in the world. Can you do that?"

He nods sheepishly.

"Right, I'm going to get her up now. I would also, please, very much like to order some ingredients to practise for a baking competition at school. I just need some things. Can I order it online, or maybe you could take me to the supermarket after we've seen Rudo later, or even after school? I also need to leave before Lolly; I've got something I need to do, which means I need you to sort her out, and where she needs to be and what she needs to have."

Dad pulls himself up and looks like he's about to say something.

"I've made her packed lunch. It's on the side."

I turn away and leave the room. I feel bad for getting angry. I try very hard to not get angry as I hate it when people are angry with me. I'm always worried that if I get angry with someone, what if something happens to them and the last thing I ever said to them was something angry or horrible or just not what I meant?

But sometimes, a bit of anger can spur you on to do things that are good for you, so long as you don't frighten anybody.

In Lolly's room I wake her up. Her hair is all puffed up and her eyes are half closed.

"Morning, Lolly!" I say. "I've made you a plate of pancakes and I love you!"

Lolly's bottom lip quivers. "Where's Mum?"

"At work. I think," I say. "It'll be OK, though. We'll see her soon."

Lolly frowns. "Why do you always get to see her and I don't? It's not fair."

I think about what she says, as I get her out of bed and find her bits and pieces of uniform. I always want the adults to be honest with me, but I make things up for Lolly all the time. Why do I do that? Is it fair? Shouldn't I just tell her the things I know too? I'm going to think about that because I want to be fair to her, and either it's OK that adults lie to me because I do it to Lolly, or it's not OK, and then it's not OK that I do it to her, either. Even if there's a good reason.

I take her by the hand and lead her downstairs. She's still frowning but when she sees the pancakes her face brightens.

"They look like Mummy's!" she says.

"She taught me everything she knows," I say. "I think I make good pancakes."

"So do I!" says Lolly, stuffing some into her mouth as I put my own sandwiches into my lunch box and make sure I have one of the greener bananas, not a brown one, because the brown ones make me feel sick, all mushy and stringy and just wrong.

Dad appears then, and says, "Wow, Lolly, glad you're enjoying breakfast. Fancy a cup of tea?"

And Lolly says, "Yes please!" and I say, "Dad what are we going to do about ingredients?" and he says, "How about you write a list when you're at school today, and I'll take you to the supermarket later, after we've been to the hospital and you've seen Rudo and Lolly's gone to the park with Odelia? How about that?"

"That sounds good," I say, and nod, put my bag on my shoulder, slip my water bottle into the side pocket, and off I go. Freedom. A bit.

When I pass number 12 I think, how can Meg live there and I've never seen her? I stop on the pavement opposite her house and look to see if anything seems out of place. What does Meg do when her mum is doing all that sawing? What if Meg is bad too, and just pretending to be nice to me so that she and her mum can saw me up? I shake my head. This is what Miss Younger would have called *letting my imagination get carried away with itself*. I heard her once, talking to another teacher. "You have to show them who's boss, is the thing. You can't be making allowances for every little tremble and tremor. That's not what the real world is like, and it's not what a school should be like either. In the real world people's little quirks are not tolerated."

And I had thought, *The real world could be like that if everyone took care of each other and accepted we are all different*. But I guess Miss Younger and me were never going to agree on anything so I'm glad I didn't bother. There are plenty of grown-ups who tolerate and celebrate little quirks. Mum is one of them. I think Mrs Locke is another.

When I get to the clubhouse I shimmy up the ladder and heave myself on to the porch, excited at having my own little morning meeting, just me. I feel quite good, despite all the things that are going on, because I've got my Great Big Family

Baking Competition to look forward to, and Dad's going to take me to the supermarket.

I make myself a cup of hot chocolate slowly, enjoying the quiet of the early morning. Part of me wants to skip school entirely and just stay here. I'd also be able to watch our house in case Mum comes back, but I know Odelia is taking me to the hospital after school, so I have to go in. I wonder if there's a way round it. Rudo would think of one.

I write my list.

Butter
Icing sugar
Self-raising flour
Plain flour
Golden caster sugar
Milk
Free-range eggs
Baking powder
Lemons
Limes
Oranges
Food colouring, many colours (natural if possible)
Marzipan
As many bags of Glacier Mints as possible.

I have a baking money box that I use to save money for ingredients. I think there's nearly forty pounds in there, and I hope that's enough. I don't expect Dad to pay for any of it. I suddenly worry that he thinks I do, and I regret not explaining it to him properly.

I've got forty-five minutes before the bus leaves for school. My plan for the day is: *School. Rudo. Baking.* I hear a car pull up outside. I'm kind of settled in to the mustard sofa, watching the way the morning light falls differently on the room through the gaps in the blinds at the windows. I can see the cars on the street, and I can see that Greg Martin is here nice and early to get the place ready for whoever he's going to push shiny houses on to today.

It's then I hear a sort of bang, and I blink and jump up, afraid I've been caught, my head racing with excuses and what will happen. I look to the door, expecting to see Greg Martin with hypnotic swirling eyes telling me I'm in big trouble. But it's not Greg Martin; it's someone else entirely. Someone I didn't expect to see in the clubhouse at all.

"Well, well, well," comes the familiar voice

from the entrance to the clubhouse. It seems like mine and Rudo's club isn't quite so secret after all.

CHAPTER
11

"Well, I heard your boyfriend's a *criminal*," says Jennifer Browne, looming over me, her silhouette totally blocking out the light. Of all the people in the world why did it have to be her? "And now it turns out you are too. Breaking and entering is a crime, you know. And this is private property."

I don't mention that she's in here too, so by her standards that makes her a criminal as well.

I gather up my things and push them into my school bag.

"I was just going," I say. I'm not going to explain myself to her or let her ruin what's going to be an amazing day.

"How dare you!" She looks really angry at that. "You know my dad is in charge of this place, don't you?" she says, not moving out of the way so I can get out. "He could cause you and your sausage roll parents a lot of trouble if I asked him to."

"I'm not sure how," I say.

"Greg. Greg Martin. That's my dad."

"He sells houses," I say, although my heart is doing that fast, loud, frightened thing inside me. "We've already bought ours."

"Pretty sure your mum and dad had to sign a thing to say they'd abide to live by some rules in the Grande Homes show home street."

I can't think of anything they've done so far that could possibly be against the rules.

"They only want nice families on these streets," she says, still standing in the doorway.

"My family is nice," I say, quietly now.

"Oh, really… Well, my dad said your mum is out and about at all hours and probably has *affairs* and all sorts of…"

I take a deep breath, wondering what on earth hypnotising-eyed Greg Martin has said about my mum. I'm ready to punch Jennifer Browne on the nose. I don't want this. I don't want to think about any of this. I want to go to school, get on with my life, and get home and bake amazing things that win me and my mum prizes.

There's another noise, and another head pokes up in the doorway.

It's Meg.

"Hullo!" she says cheerfully.

"Oh for goodness' sake," says Jennifer, crossly. "For the last time this place is *mine*, and it's not for the likes of you. Dad said I could use it. He did not say either of you could use it. Got it?"

"Did I just hear you threatening Luna?" says

Meg, still cheery. "Because it sounded like it."

"I..."

"I think you should let her past, don't you?"

"You two are the ones trespassing."

"Fine. We're trespassing," says Meg. "But now we're going to untrespass, so if you don't mind..." She nods to the doorway and then to me, and for some magical reason that I really can't work out, Jennifer steps aside so I can get out.

"Don't come back!" she calls out. "Because I'm telling my dad and you'll be in loads of trouble!"

My heart is beating fast as we climb over the back fence, scrabbling our feet and legs against the wooden panels in the hurry.

"Thank you," I say when my feet are firmly on the ground on the other side.

"No problem," says Meg. "Always a pleasure to get to confront dear Jennifer."

"How did you know about the club— I mean, tree house?"

"Ah, all the kids round here use it," she says. "Lots of us were promised them by our parents when they moved here. Turned out none of the houses actually had them."

"That's rubbish."

"It is. Too late once you're in, though."

"How come Jennifer moved out of the way for you?"

"We go a long way back," says Meg mysteriously. "She keeps out of my way, and I keep out of hers. It's a pretty good deal actually."

I stare at her in awe.

"Shall we get the bus together?" she says, smiling, and I nod and smile back. I daren't ask her about her mum. I just feel great that she's been so nice to me and that I'm standing next to someone who might want to be my friend.

CHAPTER
12

Today at school is great.

I put the application form for the Great Big Family Baking Competition in Mrs Locke's tray and she smiles at me and says, "I'm looking forward to seeing what you and your mum make," and I think, *Yes, so am I*, and feel a flutter of excitement in my belly.

At break and lunch I play with Meg, Tish and Brynn. It feels so normal and so nice that I actually feel myself let out a big rush of air that I must have been carrying around tightly inside my chest since before we moved here or something. It feels like I'm going to take off! The sun is out. There's a gentle breeze. I feel happy.

"You should come over some time," says Meg, smiling.

"You should come over too!" I say. It's the first time I've ever invited somebody to my house, even before in the mobile home. I forget to not say it, and it sort of slips out. She's smiling at me and I'm glad. I decide to take it further. "You could come over later if you like and help me practise trying to make my baking masterpiece."

"I'd love that! My mum loves baking too, but I'm just not that into it. I got a flyer and everything, but by the time I got it home I thought, nahhh, this isn't me. But, I'm a keen assistant. And I'm good at eating."

"Not sure my mum will be there," I say as casually as possible. "But I'm allowed to use the oven and stuff. Do you like marzipan?"

"I do!"

"Well, I'll buy a double amount so we can eat clumps of it as I bake!"

"I'm in. If Mum says yes," says Meg, and I feel I might burst with happiness. The rest of the afternoon whizzes by, and I even sit with Mr Waits and his group to work on my maths. Mrs Locke was right. He's very nice. He lets us use whatever equipment we like to work things out. I like round things. Beads. Counters. Little balls of plasticine. I set them out in neat lines and try to see if I can work out the answers. Sometimes I do. Sometimes I don't. Mr Waits says, "Well done, Luna. That's a really good way of doing it," and I feel like this is possibly the best day I've ever had in my life.

When Odelia comes to pick us up I can't wait to see Rudo. Lolly is excited too.

"You know Jax and Abba? Did I tell you they're

twins? Did I tell you they're having a birthday party? They are! And I'm invited. They're having bouncy castles and a chocolate fountain and a disco!" Lolly does a little shoulder dance as Odelia clicks her seat belt into the holder. We talk like that all the way, happily, and Odelia hums along to the radio.

It's good to notice moments like that. Perfect moments when nothing is going wrong, and nothing is exciting, exactly, but everyone feels content, and good. Like everything flows.

I sit at the end of Rudo's bed, while his mum goes for a walk to give us some space and Dad has taken Lolly to play at the little park in between hospital buildings. My notebook is open, ready to share everything he might need to know. It feels like so much has happened.

"How are you feeling?" I ask. I hand him the bag of practice zebra fish cake, lime and liquorice flavour, with poppy seeds in, and he says, "What on earth are these?" and I say, "Try them before you complain. I'm deep into creating a masterpiece for the family baking competition at school."

"They look like someone's cut up a zebra," he says, laughing.

"Hey! I'll have them myself if you don't want them."

"Sorry," he smiles. "They're delicious actually."

"We're going to make a fish tank," I say. "Full of brightly coloured cake fish."

"Fish cakes!" he says. "Genius!"

We nod at each other happily while he munches.

"Right, here is your update. JENNIFER BROWNE CAUGHT ME IN THE CLUBHOUSE."

Rudo leans forward in his bed. "She *what*?"

"Yup. I was in there this morning, having hot chocolate and working on my baking notes. And she sort of … turned up. Blocked me in and called us both criminals."

"Her and you?"

"No. Me and you!" I leave out the bit where she called him my boyfriend.

"Well…" He looks a bit proud at that. Then he frowns. "This means the clubhouse isn't secret any more. We can't relax in there if she's going to pop her head in. She doesn't even live in Ridgeway Close…"

"Aha!" I say. "Her dad is … wait for it…" I do

a drum roll on the bed to build tension. "Greg Martin!"

Rudo drops zebra crumbs down his hospital sheets and just stares at me. He shakes his head and his long hair ripples, like he's on an advert for expensive shampoo.

"How didn't I know that? Talk about rubbish spying." He's sitting with his mouth wide open. I can see cake crumbs on his tongue.

"I know."

"Hey! You don't have to agree with me."

"I mean me too. *I'm* rubbish at spying. I had no idea."

"This changes a lot of things..." says Rudo despondently. "I wish I wasn't stuck in here." This is the first time I've seen him upset about what's happened. He was so cheery before.

"There's something else," I say.

Rudo slumps backward and winces, pulling his hand over his bandages.

"Meg knows about the clubhouse too."

"Meg?"

"Yes. She turned up, just as Jennifer was kind of... I don't know what she was doing. She was saying things about my family..." The less I say about this the better. "Meg told Jennifer to let me go … and she sort of just did."

"Ha!" Rudo punches the air, perking up.

"Do you know why Jennifer would do whatever Meg would tell her to?"

"I think there was something in infant school," says Rudo. "They had a fight. An actual fight. Jennifer's mum was furious. Not with Meg. With Jennifer. Because she'd acted like she was … *rough* or something. She was in huge trouble. Her mum made her come in and apologise to Meg. In front of everyone."

My mind boggles at this. I can't begin to imagine it.

"They've left each other alone since."

"I can't imagine Jennifer in a fight."

"No," says Rudo. "I can imagine her enjoying starting one, though."

So can I. "Meg says all the kids in the area use the clubhouse, Rudo." I hate to break this news to him when he's stuck in bed and can't do anything about it. "It's not so secret after all."

Rudo shakes his head. "I knew it was too good to be true really."

"You're not angry?"

"I've got no right to be. I just..." He looks towards the opening in the curtain. "I just liked having a place in the world that was just for me. And for you too, obviously."

"We can find somewhere else," I say. "It doesn't have to be there."

"No," says Rudo. "I suppose not. You know anywhere that's peaceful and out of the way and no adults go to?"

I see his point. I don't. Not even slightly.

"Well, this is uplifting," he says eventually.

"Don't be sad," I say. "We'll think of something."

"We will. You're right!" His spirits seem to be lifted and I realise how happy it makes me to see him smile.

"Anyway," he says, "less about me and my beloved tree house." He says *beloved tree house* in a loud voice, like he's an actor on a stage, and it makes me laugh. "How's your mum?"

I panic then. What does he mean how's my mum? I haven't mentioned my mum. I haven't said anything is wrong with my mum. I haven't said anything about my mum other than how brilliant she is and how we're going to win this baking competition.

Then I remember his spy notebook entry. He's asking if she's OK after he saw her crying.

"She's … fine," I say at first. It's only a small lie. She probably is fine. At least I didn't say, "She's absolutely fantastic, happiest she's ever been. She just knitted me a dress of gold," which is the sort of thing I'm tempted to say when anyone asks me about her.

"Oh, good," says Rudo, smiling cheerfully. "I was worried when I overheard my mum talking about her new house. I thought you might be moving with her."

It's like I see the words come out of Rudo's mouth in slow motion. I see them, in a speech bubble, swirling about like music notes in a cartoon, up and down and around, and louder and softer, until finally, they bounce down on to his striped sheets and fall on to the floor.

"What do you mean?" I say, as calmly as possible.

"Your mum moving in with someone else must feel awful. You're dealing with it very calmly. Do you think you'll go with her? I felt bad for your dad. Dressed up all smartly with flowers to try to convince her to come home. Have you met him?

Her new boyfriend? Are you angry with her? I asked my mum and she said, 'Now, Rudo, I don't want you judging people based on a few snippets of information.' Which I took to mean I should stop talking about it." He shrugs. "Do you think you'll go with her? Will you stay in touch with me if you do? Will you go to the same school?"

I feel sick. "Dad was going to a job interview that day," I say quietly.

"Was he? Who takes flowers to an interview?" says Rudo, and even at the same time as thinking, *That's a good point*, I'm getting very angry. Being ridiculous and doing dangerous things and sneaking about might be Rudo's favourite ways to spend his time, but this is taking things too far. As if I wouldn't know about my mum moving out. Of course I would know if my mum had moved out. If she had a new boyfriend. *She hasn't moved out. There is no way on this entire planet that my mum, Dana Loveridge, aged thirty-four, from number 16 Ridgeway Close on the South Downs Estate has moved out, because she would have asked me to go with her, and Dad would have told me, and we've got the Great Big Family Baking Competition tomorrow and we are going to win it, together. She would NOT have a new boyfriend because she's married to my dad and they used to sing together in concerts and there's a photo on the living-room wall of them at their wedding.*

"Well, that's funny, *Rudo*," I say angrily, in a voice that doesn't sound like mine and must be louder than I think because he leans back in the bed and looks shocked, like he's been hit. I stand up and pulling back the privacy curtain with one big swoosh. "Because I was with her this morning in our kitchen on Ridgeway Close before school planning our bakes for the Great Big Family Baking Competition. She didn't mention ANYTHING about moving out, and seemed very happy when she kissed my dad goodbye when he went off to his new job that he got that day he went for that interview actually. So there!"

Rudo looks at me strangely, like I've said something that can't be true. *Like he's innocent*, I think, before quickly pushing that thought away.

"I…"

"And another thing," I say crossly, "I'm not sure I want to be in a secret club with someone who does criminal damage to public property and thinks it's OK to lie about someone who's supposed to be his friend's mum."

"Luna…" Rudo says. His face crumples and he looks like he might actually cry. I take one last look at his headband and his long hair and his sweet face that doesn't look like he'd be the sort of person who'd make stuff up about my mum to upset me, but the alternative is too much for me to accept.

He must be making it up. He *must be*.

With that, I turn round and storm off. I don't turn round and look back, not even when I hear his voice say, "Luna, seriously, please. I'd never lie to you." Even though it sounds like he's telling the truth. Because, you know what? People lie to you all the time. It's what people do.

CHAPTER
13

At home, once we've picked up all the ingredients from the supermarket and Dad and Lolly are playing Mario Kart in the living room, I push all the things that happened with Rudo far down inside me, because how will I ever be ready for the competition if I spend all my time between now and then thinking about it?

Rudo is lying. Or he's made a mistake. That's all there is to it.

I have to make this baking competition work. For Mum. For me.

In the kitchen I'm surrounded with flour and eggs and sugar and natural food colourings and petals from daisies and fish-shaped moulds, but nothing is going right. Every time I try to bake a batch, something goes wrong. Too wet. Too dry. The colours run. The shape doesn't set. The fish look amazing but taste like bin juice.

It's like I can't bake at all.

Mum. This is all your fault. Why don't you just come home?

My phone buzzes and I grab it quickly, thinking it must be Mum, but it's Rudo.

Why won't you talk to me? I was only telling you what I knew. I would not lie to you. OK?

I don't reply to him. I'm so cross with him. And his mum. And Dad. And my mum too. Why does nobody tell me the truth about *anything*? If nobody had lied about any of the things, I'd know what was happening and I wouldn't be making up ridiculous stories in my head that make no sense.

I bash the wooden spoon into the flour and butter and sugar and egg mix. It looks like it's started to curdle. Why today? I *can* bake. It's what I do! This is so unfair.

"Do you need any help?" I look up and there at the entrance to the dining room is Meg, with Dad and Lolly standing behind her.

"I let your friend in. Is that OK?" Dad looks nervous. There is so much I want to talk to him about, but now is not the time. I smile. "Of course! Come in!"

Meg skips over to where I'm standing while Dad and Lolly go back into the living room. She looks at the mess I've made and says, very politely, "Well, this looks interesting."

"It's a disaster!" I say, trying not to sound too desperate. "I can't make anything work. Everything I bake comes out like this." I hold out a small bowl to her full of half burnt, half wet crumbs that were supposed to be angelfish. "This has never happened to me before!"

"Do you think it's this oven?" says Meg, pointing at the oven and making me look at it with new eyes. The oven. Of course. This stupid new-house-in-a-new-estate-in-a-show-home-roll-out-road-super-swish-style oven is the problem. Not me at all. Not how I'm feeling. Not everything that's happened. This stupid, shiny chrome oven that is refusing to help me make anything that tastes or looks nice exactly when I need it to.

I kick the door of the oven, hard, with my foot, and immediately bend over clutching myself, because, *ouch*, it really hurt.

Meg runs towards me. "Are you OK?"

"You probably think I'm a psychopath now," I say, still holding tightly to my foot. "What sort of weirdo kicks an inanimate object as hard as they possibly can and maybe breaks their toe?"

The pain shoots through me and I wonder why I did such an out-of-character thing. I never get angry. I'm Miss Mellow. I'm listen-carefully-and-respond-with-a-plan person. I'm Luna Rae Loveridge and I always know what to do, and what to do never involves kicking an innocent oven just because I suddenly can't cook.

Meg puts an arm round my shoulder. "I don't think you're a psychopath. I think this cake idea is really, really ambitious and hard to do without a grown-up."

I'm about to push her hand from my shoulder and snap back that I am perfectly capable of doing it myself, but the one thing I'm sure of, which the past few days have shown me, is that I'm not perfectly capable of doing it myself. I've got myself in a muddle. And I don't know the truth of anything and I'm holding on to this cake idea as a last chance at making everything OK.

"I think you're right," I say, and lean against the kitchen counter. "But I don't actually know where my mum is, is the thing." I feel relieved to hear the words coming out of my mouth.

"You ... don't?" Meg looks me right in the eye and puts both hands on my shoulders. "Hasn't your dad told you?"

"Hasn't he told me what?"

"I don't know. Just ... where she is?"

"No," I say quietly, the flour and sugar and mess around me forgotten.

"Have you told anyone else?"

"Not really," I say. I realise what this sounds like. I'm not sure why I haven't told anyone. I could have told Mr Shaw and Miss Manning when they were asking questions. I could have told Mrs Locke when she kept proving she is *an adult I can trust*. I could have said something to Lolly every time I made a note or pancake and pretended it was from Mum. I could have told Rudo's mum Odelia ... although I think maybe she knows more about it than the others. I think I just thought I could make everything all right if I said it was all right. I thought I could keep us all together and be the perfect family, like in the brochures for the South Downs Estate, rather than the real version, which is slightly scruffy at the edges and full of sadness and mistakes and very often confusing.

"Can you talk to your dad?" Meg is spooning all the broken bits of cake and icing into the bin and clearing up for me.

"I ... could ... maybe."

"How about you do that? And how about I go and ask my mum if she wants to enter the Great Big Family Baking Competition after all, but with you, instead of me?"

I stare at her. Proper staring. Not watching. I

don't know what to say. Do I give up? Do I accept there will be no Mum to do the competition with me, and let someone else help? Or do I keep on this path I've started, where only one way of doing things will do?

I think of the catch in Rudo's voice as he called after me when I stormed away from his bed in the hospital. I feel the throb in my toe from kicking ridiculously hard at the oven door.

"If she'd like to help me, I'd like that," I say, and Meg smiles as she turns to leave and says, "Righty-ho!" and I suddenly feel so relieved that I nearly fall over.

When I hear the front door shut I go into the living room and I sit down on the sofa next to Dad and Lolly and I say, "I know you two are playing Mario Kart but I think we should talk about Mum now," and Dad says, "Ah," and Lolly says, "I know she's not been here for days, you know," and I say, "Ah," and we all look at each other as though a bubble has been burst and we've all gone tumbling on to the carpet.

"Right," says Dad. "I was hoping I could get away with not telling you. I thought I could fix it."

"That doesn't sound right," says Lolly. She's put

her controller down.

"Do you think we should talk about this in front of Lolly, Luna?"

"I think, if there's something to be known, we should both know it," I say.

All these days of me trying to create the perfect family in Lolly's eyes, trying to keep her happy, trying to give her the parents she deserved, was just as bad as Dad and Mum not telling me whatever it is that's been going on with them. You can't protect someone by making stuff up. Not forever. Not in the end.

"Mum left me," says Dad.

"She's moved in with someone else, hasn't she?" I say immediately.

He blinks with surprise but slowly nods.

"Who else? There isn't anyone else as good as us!"

Lolly looks cross and I pull her in close for a cuddle.

"It's OK," says Dad to Lolly. Then he turns to me and says, "Yes. Yes she has. She's got a boyfriend. Who isn't me." He looks very sad as he says this. Lolly is staring at us with her mouth wide open.

"You didn't go for an interview yesterday, did you, Dad?"

"No," says Dad, softly. "I went to her new house to try to get her to come home."

"What did she say?"

"She said she wasn't coming home that day or ever. And that she wants you two to be with her." He shakes his head. "I said something not good like that would never happen and then I stormed off."

I want to shout or cry or something like that, but now I've started I can't stop. "Why hasn't Mum been answering my texts?" I put my hand on my hip and look at him. I know he's not been behaving the best. I understand why, sort of, but I need him to be honest with me so I can really understand everything.

"I hid her phone," says Dad. "The first time she went to her new job. I thought if I hid her phone she'd... I don't know what I thought."

All those messages I sent her saying I loved her and she hadn't even seen them. What did she think I'd been doing? How could she just go away without saying anything or explaining anything, or putting me and Lolly in the car with her when she left and taking us with her? You can't just up and leave your children. Not if you love them.

Tears fall down my cheeks.

"I don't think I understand," says Lolly, squeezing Giraffey. "Who's been making my packed lunch?"

"I have," I say. "I didn't want you to worry."

She pulls a cross face.

"I'm sorry I didn't tell you," says Dad. "To be honest, sometimes adults don't actually know what to do. I know that's hard to believe."

I'm too polite to tell him that it's not hard to believe at all, based on his behaviour since we first decided to move house.

"Can we see her?" I say. "I want to see her. Does she want to see us?"

Dad looked ashamed. "Of course she does. It's just I said she couldn't."

I am too upset to shout at him. How dare he talk for us. I will always want to see her, no matter what she has done, and it isn't for Dad to make these decisions for me just because he's upset and angry that she doesn't want to live with him any more. Lolly starts to cry then, and I cry too, because maybe sometimes we just need to cry, because the world can be sad, and it's OK to accept it is sad, and our bodies just need to show it.

"Dad, you need to give me Mum's new number."

"I will," says Dad. "I should have never…"

"Shhh," I say. I don't want to hear his reasons and excuses. I want to think about the new information calmly until it all slots into a sort of pattern that I can understand.

Dad wipes Lolly's nose with a tissue he's got in his jeans pocket. Just as he does there's a knock at the door.

"Ah, Dad…" I say quickly. "Meg's mum lives at number twelve. She might be willing to enter the Great Big Family Baking Competition with me… That might be her. I was supposed to enter with Mum but…"

"Not a problem," says Dad, lifting Lolly up on to his hip and going to the stairs to take her up to bed. "I think Lolly needs at least three stories tonight."

"Yes!" says Lolly, punching the air. "Can we see Mum tomorrow?" she asks. "And then she can read me a story."

"I hope so," says Dad. "Now, let Meg and her mum in. I don't mind how long you stay up."

I open the door. Meg and her mum are standing there.

"Hello," says Meg's mum. She doesn't look like a mass murderer. "I'm Paula. Meg says you might need some help. I'm willing if you are…"

I nod and welcome them in. And that's how I end up standing in our kitchen with the woman from number 12 who I thought was some kind of evil villain, but who is helping me shape little fish out of sponge cake, while Meg tells me about the project they've been working on all hours of the day themselves.

"You know I said we were all promised clubhouses like the one at the show home?"

"Yes," I say, carefully grinding cardamom pods with the pestle and mortar that Mum bought for me for my tenth birthday.

"Well, Mum's been actually making me one. Of my own. To go in our garden. It's amazing. It's better than the one over there. That's all new looking and sort of fake. Mum's made it to look like a real cabin in the woods. It's amazing."

"It's not going in a tree," laughs Paula.

"There are no trees in our garden," says Meg.

"But it's nearly done! You'll have to come and see it."

"I'd love that!" I say, carefully rolling coloured balls of marzipan into the shapes of tiny stones to go at the bottom of our melted mint glass aquarium.

"Can Rudo come too?"

"Of course. Rudo is great!" says Meg.

For a moment I stop what I'm doing, wash my hands and take out my phone.

Rudo, I am so, so, so sorry for shouting at you. I was afraid. Please forgive me. My mum HAS moved in with someone new. I just didn't want to accept it because it's the saddest thing that's ever happened to me. But guess what? I've found us a new clubhouse...! X

I put a big kiss at the end and don't worry about what it looks like. Sometimes you have to make yourself look vulnerable and show others how you feel in order to make the things that matter happen. I know that now.

CHAPTER
14

It's the day of the competition and Lolly is already at school, but there's something I have to do first. I'm standing at the door of Mum's new house, with Dad waiting in the car behind me, further down the street. I knock at the door.

When Mum answers, she looks different. She's done her hair and is wearing one of her nice silk dresses. She's got those button earrings in I made her for Christmas last year.

"I entered us into a baking competition," I say quietly, still standing on the doorstep. I don't know what else to say.

"Oh, darling," says Mum. "I would love to do that with you. When is it?"

I nearly say later but I don't want to make her feel bad so I say, "Sometime in the future. There's plenty of time. Do you fancy it?" I feel it's true too. There will be time to enter baking competitions in the future. I'd made this one seem like the only important thing that would ever happen. I can't quite get myself out of trying to protect everybody yet. And I'm worried if I say the wrong thing, she'll disappear again. I've missed her so much.

"Of course I do!" She pulls me by the hand

through the door and we both put our arms round each other. "I'm so sorry that I left without saying goodbye. I thought … I thought you'd come with me the next morning, but when it came to it I couldn't do that to your dad. Before I knew it several days had gone past and I sort of…" She looks over her shoulder. "I sort of told myself you'd all be doing better without me. Not one of my best decisions, I know."

I feel cross for a moment. I'm not a toy like Giraffey to keep Dad happy. And neither is Lolly. Nobody thought to ask either of us what we wanted. I wonder about that, about how we know when our own decisions are not the best for us? I always thought being a grown-up meant that you knew how to make good decisions. How *can* we know? If I think back over the past year, two years, three years, Mum has never quite been happy at home, no matter how many sandwiches I brought her on a tray, nor how many cookies I baked. I always thought if I did enough, she'd be happy. But people don't work like that.

There are so many things I want to ask her. Why didn't she tell me she had met a new person who wasn't Dad? How long had she known him? How long had she known she wasn't going to be living with us at number 16 Ridgeway Close? How did she manage to sleep at night without having kissed me on the forehead and asked about my day? How could she just ... forget me?

"Mum..." I say. I don't know how to finish the sentence.

She's not got any nail polish on. She looks strange without it. As she leads me into the living room of her new house I realise she's put up lots of her pictures and things from the mobile home. There's her sunrise-over-the-park painting that she painted when she was a teenager, there's her poster from the concert she went to last year in the forest, with all the bands printed out in big letters. There's the mirror with the white frame, big and thick, hanging over a mantelpiece that's got the little bird ornaments she likes, and some scented candles, and her bottle of orange oil perfume, and the school photo of me and Lolly they took last year at our old school where we both look like someone's brushed our hair wrong and not quite like ourselves, mostly because the person taking the photo said, "Go on, give each other a bigger cuddle," and we looked at each other and pulled silly faces just before they took it.

The house smells like Mum. Like home.

But it smells of other things too. Washing powder that's not the one she usually uses, coming from the clean clothes hung across the radiator. There's the smell of cat food, and a cat, and I watch as a big fluffy grey animal runs across the living-room carpet.

"Oh!" Lolly and I have been asking for a cat for ages.

"Ah, that's Ursula," says Mum. "You'll like her."

"You got yourself a cat without us?" I try not to show how hurt I am, but maybe you should show people how hurt you are. I don't really know. This is all so confusing.

"It's Larry's cat," she says slowly.

"Who's Larry?" I know the answer to this before she gives it.

"He's … my new friend. He lives here too."

"I can't…" I want to say I can't believe she's moved in with a man I've never met without seeing what my opinion of him is. What if I hate him? What if he smells wrong? What if he takes all of her attention and she has none left for me or for

Lolly? What if he tries to get us to call him Dad?! I WILL hate him. I'm going to make myself hate him at every opportunity and be loyal to Dad, who's funny and kind ... and never does the laundry and has one beer too many and is grumpy in the mornings, even when Mum sets out the breakfast things nicely and says nice things to us when we come downstairs.

Grown-ups are complicated.

Is it OK to love both your parents even though both of them make terrible decisions and are not perfect like you think they are when you are really small? Because even though I'm angry with Mum and I'm angry with Dad, I know I love them, no matter what, and isn't that the strangest thing about being a human being?

"I don't want to meet him," I say firmly.

"I know," she says.

"You should have talked to me about it, so I'd understand."

"I know."

"I need to get to school"

"I know."

"Text me later," I say. "I want to hear from you. All the time. I don't want you to just disappear."

"I won't," she says. "I think you'll really like Larry. And even if you don't, I'm still your mum. Nothing ever changes that. I'm hoping you and your sister will move in here when you're ready. It'll be nice. You'll see."

Grown-ups are always saying stuff like "you'll see" and "nothing ever changes", but if there's one thing these past weeks have shown me, it's that everything changes all the time, even feelings.

She sees me edge my way back towards the door.

"Do you want a lemonade or something?"

"No thank you," I say, like I'm talking to a stranger.

"I want to explain a little bit more. Before you go. So you have something to make sense of it, and you don't start blaming yourself. I know what you're like. You know sometimes I get very, very sad?" She says this like I might not have noticed, but of course, I notice everything.

"Yes," I say.

"And you know I say it's not because of anything anyone's done, especially you and Lolly, but anyone, really. Not even Dad."

"Yes…" I say.

I never really believed that. I've always thought you can make someone happy just by doing enough of the right things; you could lift them up out of the water and hold them up, so they're in the sun. You just have to find the right way to do it. That's what I've always thought about Mum. *If I just find the right thing to make her never sad again.*

"It really isn't because of anything anyone does or doesn't do," she says softly. "It's just … brains. They sometimes don't work properly and people feel like … everything about them is not good and they just can't live the old way any more. Even if they have people who love them. Even if they have lots of things to look forward to. It's a mystery really. How it happens and who it happens to. It's nobody's fault."

"Is that what happened?" I say. "Did you not want to be here any more?"

Mum puts her hand in my hair and strokes it. "Yes. Sort of," she says. "I just knew if I stayed being in a couple with your dad one day I would feel like that. Living with him was making me poorly. Not him. Not you or Lolly. The situation. I tried. I really did."

"How can you forget us at times like that?" I say, my eyes hot with tears. "How can you forget *me*?"

"I don't forget you, Luna," she says in a voice that almost sounds like she's singing. "At times like that I think you'd be better off without me."

"No!" I shout then. "NEVER, NEVER, NEVER! Mum, NEVER! I'd NEVER be better off without you. EVER."

"I know, love," she says. She strokes my hair and I feel really small, like I did when I was a toddler and she'd sing me to sleep.

"You're not coming home, are you?"

"No, love." She shakes her head and gives me another little smile.

"You'll let me visit you, though, won't you?" I ask, and panic at the thought that she might not. "When … Larry … isn't here? And we can go into town. And we can still bake together?"

"Of course I will," she says. "Don't be too angry with your dad. He thought he was protecting you. It's not an easy conversation to have with a small person."

"I'm not very small," I say.

"You know what I mean." I think of how I say things to Lolly to make life easier for her, to make her happy, to take away any worries that might make her day harder, and I nod. Just a little.

I stare at her. Is there really nothing I can do? No magic potion? No cake that's big or lemony or beautiful enough? Is there nothing a person can do to make another person want to be with them? Nothing at all? Can I really not make Mum love Dad the way I'd like her to? I want to be able to make it all better. But maybe human beings don't work that way. I think of the past week. Everything I've done to try to make things better on my own have gone wrong. Maybe Mum's right after all. Maybe it's not all down to me.

"Do you understand?" I can feel her breath on my neck.

I nod my head slightly. "Why does nobody ever tell kids stuff like this?" I say.

"I think they think it will frighten you," she says. "I think they want to hide all the bad things in the world away from you so you can enjoy being young and happy."

"I can't enjoy being young and happy if the adults are always forcing me to be a detective," I say. "Not if they don't tell me the truth."

"I know," she says softly. "I went about this all wonky."

I smile at the word, *wonky*.

"I think grown-ups should tell kids about these things sometimes," I say. "Because otherwise if it ever happens to them when *they're* grown-ups, they'll feel like the only ones in the world, like there's something really wrong with them, and it might make them feel even worse."

"That's a good point," says Mum.

"There's nothing worse than feeling like you're the only one in the world," I say.

I think of Meg's mum, helping me weigh out the flour, and I think of Meg, putting her hand on my shoulder after I kicked the oven, and I think, *I am not the only one in the world.* I think of Rudo, smiling at me that first day as we climbed over the fence to the show-home garden. I think of Dad, with his smoothed-down hair and his bunches of gladioli who I love very much, but can't imagine how difficult it would be to be married to him. I think of Lolly, laughing, with her tongue up her nose.

"No, there isn't," says Mum, agreeing.

"You're not the only one in the world, Mum," I say, patting her on the leg.

"I know, darling. And I hope you know I love you very much. You're not the only one in the world either."

"I'm glad," I say. "I really missed you. I thought you'd run away because I was so terrible at being your kid."

Mum takes in a deep breath and pulls me closer.

"I'm sorry you thought I'd just run away because I didn't love you. That's the very opposite of how I feel. I love you so much sometimes it fills me up entirely."

I think very carefully before I reply to this. My head is full of all the gaps in things, all the secrets and all the pretending, and how each of us fills up the gaps with our own worries or fears and the worst thing we could possibly think of, and how so often those things are totally wrong and make everything you see around you off balance and … wonky.

"Can you promise me one thing, Mum?" I hold her hand. It's so good to have the feel of her near me.

"Can you promise to tell me stuff as it is, instead

of making things up to make it easier at the time? It doesn't make it easier. It makes everything much more confusing. It makes me think all sorts of things that make life seem worse."

She nods and smiles. "I can promise that," she says softly. "I've never thought of it like that."

"Good," I say and give her a hug. "I really need to go to school now. I'll text you later."

"That would be lovely," Mum says.

"I'll see you tomorrow," I say as she opens the door and I step out into this new world where I don't even live with my own mum. "I love you."

"Love you too," she says, and I feel her watching me as I walk down the street to get into Dad's car, but I just can't turn round to look at her as I might not manage to walk any further. She might not be able to help me win the Great Big Family Baking Competition, but she's still my brilliant mum.

CHAPTER
15

I look at my phone and read Rudo's message. Good luck today, I know you can do it!

I'm so glad he forgave me for shouting at him and calling him a liar.

THANK YOU! I type back. I'll bring you some cake later.

In the bags I have everything I need as I enter the school hall and take a big breath. I look up. Meg's mum is already at our table, with an apron on and a chef's hat and she's smiling at me, a big, wide grin.

"Right!" she says eagerly. "Let's win this thing. Don't forget, you're in charge.

I get out everything I've brought with me, and together we set it out. There's all the sponge cake we made last night, and a tub of multicoloured marzipan stones. My experiment with the Glacier Mint sheets went brilliantly. Nearly. There are three perfect rectangles, shiny and clear, and one that's slightly bobbled and curled up at the edges.

"I'm sure we can make a fish tank out of this," says Meg's mum generously. I laugh. Where did being a perfectionist ever get me? Together we make the tank out of the pieces and set up all the things inside. I cut my gingerbread bricks into neat shapes, and cement them with lime butter icing until they make a tall, round castle rising up inside the tank. My original idea to have the fish hanging just wouldn't work, but I love Paula's idea to slide them down on wooden kebab sticks, which she's painted blue with food colouring. We stick the sticks into the marzipan pebbles and put the fish at different heights. At the very last minute we spin sugar to look like seaweed and aquatic plants and step back to look at our creation,

All around us the hall is buzzing with activity. Ours looks nothing like the designs in my notebook, nothing like the perfect, lifelike fish tank full of coloured fish I'd imagined when I started out. It looks better. It looks like we made it as a team. It looks like two actual human beings have made it, and like they've had fun doing it. It doesn't look perfect.

That's the thing. When I first heard of the competition I didn't once wonder if it would be fun. I forgot about the fun completely. I look up at Paula and over at Meg who's sitting at the side with Rudo's mum and my dad and Lolly and I think, *OK, this was fun.*

"Not bad, not bad," says Paula, smiling.

"Not bad at all," I say. "I reckon my mum would love this."

"I'm sure she would."

I could have told Mum about it being today. I could have had her come with me. But I'm not ready. Not yet.

I look over at Jennifer Browne and her mum, who looks nothing like the woman of my imagination. They've made a big mermaid cake, with long dark hair, and a big sponge cake tail covered in hundreds of homemade fondant-icing scales. They're just applying a silver spray to the tail. It looks magnificent; there's no other word for it. In an ideal world me and Meg's mum would win and Jennifer's cake would fall apart and taste disgusting.

But it's not an ideal world.

And of course they win first prize. And of course Jennifer Browne pulls a smug look and flicks her hair at me, and of course she's noticed my mum isn't even there, but none of that really matters any more.

Because I'm really proud of what we've made.

I'm even prouder when one of the judges – a

school governor – comes round and puts a little Highly Commended sticker beside our fish tank creation. We haven't come first. But still. Someone noticed us!

"What a wonderful idea," the judge says, smiling. "I love your sense of adventure!" I puff up with pride at that and I look over to see the others clapping wildly. Sometimes you don't get first prize. You get something else instead. A feeling.

On the way home Dad gives me Mum's new mobile number and I type it into my phone so I can send her a message later.

"There's lots to talk about, Luna," he says apologetically.

"There is," I say. "But not today."

Meg's mum invites me round for tea and because Dad has a party to take Lolly to, he says yes and we rush straight over to number 12, the house that had so creepily caught my imagination on our first night here. There are no dead bodies. There's just a nice house and a brilliant clubhouse that Meg and her mum have made from scratch.

It looks like the gingerbread cottage from a fairy story. It's got a blue-tiled roof and proper windows. There is a chimney (but no working fire, obviously), and inside there's a table, chairs, a sofa, an armchair and a shelf of books and games. There are things for colouring and painting set out on the table. There's a radio, which Meg turns on as I slump down on to a brightly coloured beanbag.

"Do I ever have to get up from here?" I ask.

"Not if you don't want to," laughs Meg. "This is our clubhouse now."

We eat the little cakes in the shape of colourful fish and put our feet up on the sofa, and we hum along to the songs on the radio.

"I can't believe you and your mum made this!" I say, shaking my head. It might not be in a tree. It might not have all the designer touches the show home one had, but it has something even better. It has *us* in it. And we don't have to sneak about. It's been made especially for us. By someone who understands that kids need a place in the world with no adults around.

"I can't wait till Rudo sees this," I say, and I send him a photo of our feet up and the cakes in our hands. Get well soon X

You got it x comes Rudo's immediate reply. Sooner than you think!

My mum lives in a house up the road with a man I've never met and not with me. My best friend is in hospital. My dad needs to find a job and start taking care of himself again. Nobody is cheering for me winning the Great Big Family Baking Competition because I didn't win it, and there are no headlines about NEW GIRL SAVES THE DAY, or NEW GIRL BAKES THE MOST IMPRESSIVE FISH CAKES OF ALL TIME IN BAKING COMPETITION SHOWDOWN AND SCHOOL BULLY DISSOLVES IN FREAK LIGHTNING STRIKE.

This is real life after all.

Meg's mum knocks at the door. "I know it's kids only in there," she says, laughing, "but I've just had Greg Martin at the door."

I look at Meg and she looks at me. We push open the new clubhouse door.

"He said two things. One, nobody will be going in the tree house at number thirty any more."

"We know," I say. "It's illegal."

"Well, it certainly is now," she says. "Somebody's bought the house and the show home is moving further on, to one of the houses on one of the other newly finished streets further along, past the park area."

"You mean someone's going to finally have the tree house for real?" Meg shakes her head. "That's one lucky kid."

"Nope," laughs her mum. "He informs me that it's being taken down and reassembled in the garden of the new show house. He said to say if any of you are caught in the new one, he'll be forced to take action."

"Why would we want to go in there?" I say, crossly.

"Exactly," says Meg.

"I told him of course you would stay well away and wished him a good day."

"You did?"

"I did."

"Thanks, Mum," says Meg.

"You're welcome. I'm going inside to watch TV. Just shout if you need anything."

"Will do," says Meg.

"Thank you for today," I say, and give the biggest smile I can possibly muster.

"Any time," she says, and heads back towards

the house.

Meg pushes the door closed and turns on one of the lamps. I look at my phone. Dad has sent a photo of Lolly at the birthday party. There's a row, of her, Jax and Abba. They all have their tongues, nearly, up their noses. I laugh. Some things are just as they should be.

I finally send a text to my mum on her new number.

Love you, Mum xxx

I push more cake into my mouth and take a sip of lemonade.

Meg laughs and gets out a sheet of paper. "RIGHT," she says with a grin. "Is this a spying-on-people club or what? What do you think about the couple in flat ten? Because I'm thinking they're definitely hiding something." She writes *alien tendencies* above a picture she's beginning to do of their flat. Round it she draws a map of our street, and I let out a big, happy breath.

"I've been thinking about that woman at number two, too. Have you noticed anything odd about her?" Meg draws a big question mark above a little sketch of the woman's house.

"I have!" I say. "Have you noticed she puts

all her rubbish in her recycling bin, and all her recycling in her rubbish bin?"

"No!" says Meg. "I haven't! What do you think it means…?"

"I try not to jump to conclusions these days," I say. "Seeing as I thought your mum was some kind of axe murderer."

Meg laughs. "Is there anything else about her?"

"She lets her dog wear a little jacket with a collar. Like he's going to work in the city."

Meg falls about laughing. "Wait till you see him in the Hawaiian shirt she puts him in, in summer. Never knowingly underdressed is that dog." She writes *bin confusions*, and *overdressed canine* above the house in tiny writing.

There's a knock at the clubhouse door, and when we open it, Rudo is standing there, his backpack on his back as usual.

"Rudo!" I say, leaping up and nearly knocking him over as I go to hug him. He winces and I pull back in case I've hurt him.

"You don't think I'd miss out on this, do you?" he says, pulling me back over and giving me a squeeze. "Now who's for some sneaking…?"

"*Safe* sneaking…" I say.

"Of course," he laughs. "Who do you think I am?"

He sits on the corner of one of the armchairs and all three of us huddle round the map of Ridgeway Close. There's a lot of spying to be done, lots of secrets to uncover, and I'm going to enjoy every single minute of it.

Just then, my phone buzzes with a reply from Mum.

I love you too, Luna. Hope I see you tomorrow xxx

She *will* see me tomorrow. And every day after that. Because nobody is going to let me think my mum has upped and left me again. I'm still going to worry about things. I'm still *me*. I'm just going to worry about them in front of other people, so they can tell me when I'm being silly, or when I've got it wrong, or just put their hands on my shoulder when I kick an oven in frustration and make me feel better. Not that I'm going to be doing that again in a hurry. My toe is killing me. I'm not going to blame myself for what's been going on between my mum and dad right in front of my nose for ages either.

"Right," says Meg. "What about that man at number seventeen?"

"The one who has his shopping delivered when it's really late at night?" says Rudo.

"Yes! He does!"

"What do you think he's buying? Secret supplies for a revolution?"

"Secret supplies for prisoners he's keeping in his cellar?"

"Two thousand boxes of eggs for an attempt at the world record for making the most omelettes in a five-hour time frame?"

The conversation continues like this and I feel happy.

The thing about a new house is everything's *new*.

That sounds really obvious, I know, but if you think about it, one of the things about where you live is that you build up all this stuff there. And not just stuff, *memories* linked to stuff. All the little ways things work, like the handle you had to push down twice to get into the bathroom, or the groove on the front step that if you went over it too fast you'd trip and land splat on your front. Or how far to open the window to let in enough fresh air so you can fall asleep but nobody could ever get in. Or the *smell*.

Good smells: Meg's clubhouse, Glacier Mints melting in the pan, baking.

Bad smells: secrets.

You get used to old things.

New things take getting used to.

New people do too.

This time I think I can get used to them.

ACKNOWLEDGEMENTS

Many people are involved in the making of a book. Thank you to everyone who's helped bring Luna's story to life. Especially editor and cake provider extraordinaire Tom Bonnick. I appreciate everything you've done and working with you was so easy it was a dream. Thank you to superagent Jo Unwin, and Kate Wilson from Nosy Crow too. I can't think of a better home for this book.

A shout out to all the pupils and staff at Fakenham Junior School – and especially to the 2019-2020 Year 6 Reading Club that never finished the books we wanted to because of COVID-19 lockdown. I loved all the sessions we did and will always remember them. I hope you all keep reading and writing. You're brilliant. Thank you to Kestrel class. How lucky I am to be your teacher!

Thanks to Holly Seddon, Will Dean, Owen Booth, Keris Stainton, Alice Broadway and Rachael Lucas for reading earlier drafts which were different, but at the heart, the same. Your friendship and encouragement of all my writing means so much to me. Thank you to the other kids who grew up on Rudland Close and thought it would be a good idea to play in the show home garden.

Thank you to my sister, Jodie. Helping look after you helped me look after myself. And now we look after each other. To all my friends. Luna Rae often feels alone. I don't and that's because of all of you.

Thank you Nell. You are an absolute star, I love you. Never forget that being yourself is enough. Everything I write is for you, so you never have to doubt how important you are to me. Being your mum is the best thing that has ever happened to me.

Last thank you, to you for reading this book. We need to keep our eyes out for the Lunas. We need to make sure nobody feels alone.